THE LAND OF ELYON BOOK I

THE DARK HILLS DIVIDE

Patrick Carman

AMPED MEDIA
WALLA WALLA

The Land of Elyon
Book I
The Dark Hills Divide

Third Printing
April 2004

ISBN 0-9742287-0-2

Amped Media
22 Shaw Place
Walla Walla, Washington 99362

Write to us at
letters@landofelyon.com

Visit us on the web at
www.landofelyon.com

Printed in the United States of America

For Karen

PART I

"*At every locality where ocean meets land there are the cliffs of dark jagged rocks. If you look over the edge there lies a mist a few feet below; so thick you can't see the water. As far as the eye can see, nothing but white, puffy mist, as if we hang in the clouds and to step off the edge would leave us falling for days. If not for the violent sound of the waves against the rocks somewhere far below, one might suppose our lands were an island in the sky.*"

Beyond the Valley of Thorns,
Alexa Daley

Before I built a wall I'd ask to know
What I was walling in or walling out,
And to whom I was like to give offense.
Something there is that doesn't love a wall,
That wants it down.

Mending Wall,
Robert Frost

Warvold

"Stop that chattering or we'll have to go back and sit by the fire," said my companion. He removed his large, thick cape and draped it over my shoulders. I had to hold it up to keep it from dragging on the street, but it felt good, and my last few shivers quietly subsided.

The sun had set, and the lamps glowed above the streets with sharp yellow spears, one every twenty feet on both sides along our way. The cobblestone paths lined with homes and gates, illuminated by the soft light, made for a dreamy stroll. As we rounded each new corner we were greeted by another twisting row of lamps with more houses and small storefronts. Some of the doors were painted bright blue or purple, but the houses themselves, crammed tightly together, were all white-washed stone.

We walked together, not saying a word. The town was quiet but for the occasional distant hoot of a night owl from its perch atop the wall as it searched for rats and other vermin. We arrived at the end of a darkened footpath to a locked iron gate. He produced a golden key from his pocket and drew it to a small oval container hanging from a chain around his neck—a locket I had seen many times. I watched as he opened the container and removed another key, inserted it into the lock on the gate, and swung the gate wide open on rusty hinges.

He disappeared into the darkness, calling me to follow quietly. I groped for his hand, which he took in his, and we walked farther, his cape now dragging behind me. He stopped, took my hand out of his, opened it full, and pulled it forward until I felt the smooth surface of rock still warm from the days cooking. Reaching as high as I could, I felt a seam, and then more rock.

"It's the wall," he said. "I thought you might enjoy touching it." Except for his breathing, I heard nothing. After a while, he continued: "I spent my youth building this wall to keep dangerous things away. I sometimes wonder now if I've kept them inside."

"Why would you say that?" I could make out his features as my eyes adjusted to the darkness. He was deep in thought, staring at the wall as he ran his delicate fingers along the seam. Lines ran all along his weathered face, and the hair from his head and beard tangled together into a fluffy white mass.

"I tell you what, Alexa, why don't we sit a spell and I'll tell you a tale. We need to stay low or old Kotcher will get his dogs to come looking for a nibble."

He had a reputation for conjuring up frightening tales about giant spiders crawling over the wall to eat children, so naturally I was concerned. "What sort of a story are you going to tell?"

"Actually, it's more of a fable. I heard it a long time ago, during my travels, before all this," and he swept his hand in front of him, a far off look in his eye. "Most people don't know how much I traveled when I was young. I walked for miles and miles in every direction for months on end, all alone.

"But then Renny and Nicholas came along, and I grew more and more protective. I had terrible fears of being away from them; so I stayed closer to home. Before long I was building these walls to protect my family and everyone else."

Both of us were sitting now, and he looked me in the eye as he continued, "You remember one thing, Alexa. If you make something your life's work, make sure it's something you can feel good about when you're an old relic like me." He paused, either for effect or because he had forgotten what he was going to say next, I wasn't sure which.

"When I was on one of my far off journeys, I heard this fable. I liked it so much I memorized it." And then he told it to me, and it went like this:

"It was six men of Indostan
To learning much inclined,
Who went to see the Elephant,
Though all of them were blind,
That each by observation might satisfy his mind.

The First approached the Elephant,
And happening to fall
Against his broad and sturdy side,
At once began to bawl:
'God bless me! But the Elephant
Is very like a wall!'

The Second, feeling of the tusk,
Cried, 'Ho! What have we here?
So very round and smooth and sharp?
To me 'tis mighty clear
This wonder of an Elephant
Is very like a spear!'

The Third approached the animal,
And happening to take
The squirming trunk within his hands,
Thus boldly up and spake:
'I see,' said he, 'the Elephant
Is very like a snake!'

The Fourth reached out an eager hand,
And felt about the knee.
'What most this wondrous beast is like is mighty plain,' said he;
"Tis clear enough the Elephant is very like a tree.'

The Fifth who chanced to touch the ear,
Said: 'Even the blindest man
Can tell what this resembles most;
Deny the fact who can,
This marvel of an Elephant
Is very like a fan!'

The Sixth no sooner had begun
About the beast to grope,
Than, seizing on the swinging tail
That fell within his scope,
'I see,' said he, 'the Elephant
Is very like a rope!'

And so these men of Indostan
Disputed loud and long,
Each in his own opinion
Exceeding stiff and strong,
Though each was partly in the right
And all were in the wrong.

"Not bad for an absentminded old man," he said.

"Stop being so gloomy. I think you've got a fine memory."

"A lot of secrets are held inside these walls, a lot more are roaming around outside," he said. "I think the two are about to meet."

He mumbled something else about "them being right all along," but he was quieter now, muttering to himself.

We sat and listened to the soft evening wind blow in, and

then I started shivering again. "I'm getting cold, can we go now?" He gave me no reply, and as I glanced up at him on that clear, cold night, it was obvious that Warvold was dead.

THE ROAD TO BRIDEWELL

I'm twelve years old, short for my age, with skinny arms and knobby knees. My father often jokes that he could run my forearm through his wedding ring (sadly, this is only a slight exaggeration). I have sandy colored hair, which I keep in a ponytail nearly all the time. My name is Alexa, and my father is the mayor of the town I live in.

A few hours before Warvold's death, I was traveling with my father from our hometown of Lathbury to Bridewell. Being a girl of twelve and lacking adventure, the annual trip was the most anticipated time of the year for me. It had been a quiet day on the road, though hot beyond belief for so early in the summer.

In Bridewell there is a building, which at one time was a prison. A work camp really, where the vagrants and the misfits from our towns used to be kept. During the day, the prisoners would go outside the wall, doing hard labor of one sort or another.

When I say wall, I do not mean the prison wall, although that wall does exist. The wall I am speaking of is the one that surrounds all of Bridewell, which encircles not only the small village and the old prison, but stretches out along each side of the roads leading to the three cities of Lathbury, Turlock, and Lunenburg. Our kingdom is a wagon wheel made of stone with

Bridewell at its hub, the three towns on the end of the three spokes. On the afternoon before Warvold's death, we were traveling on the Lathbury spoke on our way to Bridewell.

The walls loomed above us on both sides of the road, holding in the heat like a long, skinny oven, and I was hot and bored.

"Father?"

"Yes?"

"Tell me the story of when they built the walls."

"Haven't you grown tired of that old legend yet?" Of course, I knew very well he enjoyed telling it. My father had a great love of storytelling, and this was one of his favorites. I didn't have to wait long for him to begin.

"Thomas Warvold was an orphan. On the day of his thirteenth birthday he wandered off from his hometown, all of his belongings stored in a single knapsack. For years no one knew or cared where he'd gone. A seemingly worthless child with no parents and no future to speak of; it's doubtful anyone even noticed he had departed. But he was a spirited boy, smart, and full of adventure. Much later, after he became famous, there were those that speculated he was an aimless wanderer for twenty years or more, gathering treasures of various sorts from far off places in the Land of Elyon. Others suggested he lived in the wilds of the enchanted forests and mountains beyond these very walls. In any case, it would seem that he grew to be a forceful leader, for eventually he convinced others to join him in a place most everyone believed was haunted, dark, and dangerous."

The sound of horse claps echoed off the towering walls as we advanced on Bridewell, and my father paused to scratch the golden stubble on his chin. He was a big man with red hair, long and twisted and tangled. In the winter he wore a beard, but the summers proved too much for him and he took solace in the cool relief of a shaven face.

"As Warvold began to thrive and prosper, more people became convinced that the area was indeed safe to live in, and so they came. The valley where Warvold first settled, which is now called Lunenburg, eventually filled up to capacity and provided no room for growth. Lunenburg was in more of a crevice than a valley. High mountains rose on either side. On one end of the tight valley was the already established town of Ainsworth, on the other, the uncharted dangers and scary legends of the wilderness. When yet more families moved into the town, Warvold decided it was time to expand.

"Once out of the valley the north held giant mountains, the east a thick forest; the west was covered in what came to be known as The Dark Hills. The people of Lunenburg were afraid to venture out past the valley and into the wild.

"It was then that Thomas Warvold had a most wonderful idea."

My father stopped talking as a cart passed ours, kicking up dust with its two horses.

"Dear me, so sorry Mr. Daley. I didn't realize…," the driver stammered. He was upset about carelessly overtaking the mayor of Lathbury and his daughter.

His carriage was almost past ours when my father whipped our two horses and yelled out, "Hya! Hya!" We quickly came neck and neck with the other cart, leaving about three feet between us, and three feet at either side of the wall. My father gave the rival driver a wicked look and proclaimed, "I've not lost a race on the road to Bridewell in five years!"

I was almost thrown from my seat with a thrust of the powerful horses as the race plunged into action. Our opponent, frothing with excitement at racing someone as important as my father, stayed with us for quite a long time. Dust filled the air and the furious sound of hooves and wheels churned down the road to Bridewell.

The walls flew past us, stretching into the sky for what

seemed like miles. In reality, they were forty-feet up, three feet wide, and made of three-foot-square-stone blocks. The walls run the ten-mile distance from Lathbury to Bridewell, and the same from Lunenburg and Turlock; thirty miles of walled road in all, plus another two miles around Bridewell.

Lathbury and Turlock are butted up and walled in against the lonely sea where fierce, mist covered waves break against the soaring cliffs. The River Roland also runs through these parts, so named for the only man known to have crossed it (a man who no one has seen or heard from since). The river is a wide and powerful mass of fast moving water, fed by mountains in yet uncharted lands. As for Lunenburg, it is but a few miles from the larger city of Ainsworth, thus completing the fortress of total safety and comfort around our kingdom.

Lost in my thoughts, I had taken my attention away from the race. When my father pulled hard on the reins to slow the horses, my slight frame nearly flew forward off the cart.

"What a pleasant diversion," my father proclaimed as the challenger trotted his horses up beside us, covered from head to toe in a thick coat of dirt. "A shame about the dust."

"Quite all right sir, quite all right. My horses are not what they used to be, but they gave it all they had," the man said. He was doing his best to shake off while we continued down the road.

"What brings you to Bridewell on this wretched hot day?" my father questioned.

"Actually, I'm off to Turlock, delivering the weekly mail from Lathbury."

"Have you a name?" said my father.

"Silas Hardy, at your service." He was finished dusting himself off, and smiled back at us with bright-white teeth against a darkly tanned face.

"Well Silas, how about you escort us the rest of the way to Bridewell? I wouldn't want to leave you behind with those unreliable animals dragging you into town. Besides, I'm just telling my daughter about the wall and how it was built. An enjoyable story you might just as well sit in on."

Silas looked up at the walls on both sides and the hot sun above, beads of sweat running down his temples.

"I've heard it many times sir, but I'm hot and bored and my horses are too tired to outrun you. Let's hear it again." He wiped the sweat from his temple and rested his elbows on his knees, holding the reigns loosely in his large, meaty hands.

"As I was saying before our new friend Silas joined us, Warvold had a problem. More people were immigrating to the area: pioneers, miners, merchants, and families. Many came to the valley looking for a better life, and the poor little town quickly became overcrowded.

"Then one day Warvold had an idea. A *tremendous* idea. He would build a walled road ten miles out into the unknown, and there he would build a new town. As long as the wall was in front of the people, the enchanted dangers that lurked about could be kept away." And then with a comical dark look, my father added, "Only, who would build the wall? Surely the people of Lunenburg were too afraid to stand outside, or near the edge, which is what would be required to build such a thing.

"No, Warvold needed other people to do the work. And so he met with the leaders of Ainsworth, a large city, five miles away, from which he had originated.

"Ainsworth had a prison that held the pickpockets, vagrants, and disobedient servants—petty criminals mostly. Before they were thrown in prison, many were homeless and were found sleeping in chicken houses or haystacks.

"In that town, if you were found to be loitering or begging for a period of five days in a row, you were brought before two justices, marked with a hot iron on the breast with a 'V' for vagabond, and sent to the prison to perform hard labor."

A red-tailed hawk flew low overhead, and another sat upon

the top of the crusted wall to my right. This was a common sight as hawks were always about the walls, and more appeared as we drew nearer to the city gate.

"Warvold made a deal with the leaders of Ainsworth," my father continued. "He was building a prison in Lunenburg, had been for some time, and he was willing to take three hundred of the foulest vagabonds Ainsworth had to offer. There was but one condition: after ten years, Warvold could return the vagabonds to Ainsworth, no questions asked.

"The leaders of Ainsworth thought this was a wonderful idea. Their own prison only held four hundred men, and was full to capacity. Giving the vagabonds to Warvold allowed them time to plan a new, larger prison. And besides, they agreed that most of the vagabonds would die or return so weak they could be sold as harmless servants to the local farmers.

"The deal was done, and within a year, the Lunenburg prison was complete and the vagabonds delivered as promised. Warvold was not one to take chances, so he devised a plan of his own to make sure the vagabonds never escaped unnoticed. As slaves to Lunenburg, Warvold branded each vagabond with an 'S' on the forehead or ball of the cheek, thus making clear to everyone in Lunenburg who was slave and who was free.

"The rest is as I've told you a hundred times, Alexa," said my father. "Warvold put the vagabonds to work, and in three years they built the wall to what is now Bridewell. By that time, more people flooded into the valley, and when the walled road was completed, Lunenburg popped like a cork from a bottle of sour wine. People streamed out of it to settle Bridewell, and many even helped build the two miles of wall that now surrounds the city. As quick as the wall around Bridewell was complete, two more walled roads were started by the vaga-bonds under Warvold's lead. Over the next several years the ten-mile walled roads to Turlock and Lathbury were finished, thus completing our kingdom. Four cities, Bridewell as the hub; Lunenburg, Lathbury, and Turlock its spokes.

"The kingdom of Bridewell Common, now complete, had no use of the vagabonds, and Warvold returned them to Ainsworth as he promised. Even with the hard labor, Warvold was a decent man, and took good care of the three hundred slaves. Seven years ago, he returned all except a handful that had died of disease or injury." With that, my father was finished.

And we were at the gate to Bridewell.

BRIDEWELL

B ridewell is the center of everything in our small universe. It has three gates; just like the one we entered this afternoon, one gate for each walled road. Each gate is made of solid oak and iron. The gates are raised and lowered by chains with thick metal links the size of a horse's head. Towers flank each gate where guards observe everyone entering and leaving the encircled town.

"Raise the Lathbury gate!" Yelled the guard atop the lookout to our left. "Mr. Daley has arrived."

The gate creaked ominously before us, stalled, and then burst back to life. It roared open, the chains grating against the stone wall, and the town crept into view as the sun hit the earth in front of us. I crouched down to see under the rising gate, and then I rose up along with the giant groaning door as the inside of Bridewell came into full view.

It was just as I had remembered it: full of tightly packed houses and buildings crisscrossed by narrow streets. Not a single house was constructed more than two stories high, so none were tall enough to look out over the wall. The houses and the streets were simple, well kept, and crafted with extraordinary care. The homes were a mix of stone and wood: stone for the walls, aged-hardwood for the doors and windowsills, and wood shingles for the roofs. The roads and walkways were cobblestone, worn to a rustic brown but free of garbage and debris.

In the distance I saw the one building that was a full three stories, which peeked just over the west side of the barrier between the town and The Dark Hills outside. This was the old prison building, a place where I had slept, eaten my meals, and looked for secrets in the many rooms and passageways.

Once the vagabonds had been returned to Ainsworth, there was no longer a need for a prison in Bridewell. It had been converted, renamed Renny Lodge, and was currently home to a library, two courts, and several classrooms for art masters and apprentices of various trades. A portion of the large building was also devoted to the annual meeting we had come to attend. Fancy rooms for boarding, a large kitchen and dining area, a meeting room for official business, and a smoking room with a large fireplace (though hot during the day, it was cold at night in Bridewell, and a late fire was common even in summer months). The basement contained a musty old cellblock, hardly ever used except as a holding area for prisoners transported from town to town.

We were a simple, passive society and we generally kept to ourselves, but the summers were a time of trade for our craftsmen and craftswomen. In addition to the usual doctors, blacksmiths, storekeepers and such, each of our towns housed facilities for bookmaking and repairing. We were known in Ainsworth as the finest and most reliable creators of ornate covers and sturdy spines; and it was said far and wide that we were a people skilled at the task of restoring the most treasured books and manuscripts.

In the heat of summer many of the inhabitants of Bridewell were in Ainsworth or other parts of our kingdom collecting damaged books for repair, taking on new projects, delivering finished volumes, and otherwise attending to the trade business of our society. It was our time to move about and 'set up shop' in Ainsworth. Visitors from far away towns would come and collect finished works. Often they brought along more books for repair and written manuscripts for setting in type and developing into finished books. With so many of our inhabitants traveling and working elsewhere, summer in Bridewell was calm: few people, an occasional quiet breeze, clean and tidy and ideal for exploring.

We approached the ponderous square mass of Renny Lodge and lurched to a stop. I was immediately down on the hard stone drive, glad to be free of the bumpy ride. A servant emerged and took my father's bags, I kept my own, and we walked the few steps up to the entryway. I hopped on each, counting as I went, *one, two, three,* and entered the stone building.

Renny Lodge was chopped up into several sections. The entryway was a large open space with a hallway leading to first floor classrooms, courtrooms, and apprentice chambers. Red velvet drapes were pulled back from the windows, and a dust filled streak of sunlight poured onto the wood staircase leading to the second floor. Another set of stairs, hidden in the shadows, led down to the cellblock.

"Oh dear me, it *is* hot today. I imagine it only gets hotter as we get higher. Up we go!" said my father. He was bounding up the stairs ahead of me, two steps at a time. I scurried after him, pulling myself up by the banister, just catching his shirttail as we arrived at the top.

My father was prone to grand entrances, and he burst into the smoking room with both arms raised, clamoring for a hug from anyone who would offer one to a weary traveler.

"Well if it isn't my favorite little lady!" came a voice, completely ignoring my father and whisking me into his arms. It was Ganesh, the mayor of Turlock, an amusing and lively man with a dry wit and a grandfatherly love for almost everyone he encountered. If Warvold was the brains of Bridewell, then Ganesh was its heart.

"It's so dry around here the trees are bribing the dogs," he said, his full black beard tickling my bare shoulder.

Our dash up the stairs had landed us on the backside of the building in the smoking room. It was easily the most comfortable place in Renny Lodge. Lots of large windows adorned with velvet drapes, this time purple, filled the room with cheery light, and beautiful furniture was placed comfortably on ornate throw rugs. An imposing rock fireplace, surrounded by inviting couches and chairs, took up one wall. On another wall were double doors leading into the official meeting room.

I glanced over Ganesh's shoulder and saw Warvold, his weary old body crumpled in a heap on a plush red chair. He smiled at me and winked, then reached his arm out towards me. Ganesh set me back on the wood floor, looked my father up and down, and said, "James Daley! Still as full of wind as a corn-eating horse?"

Ganesh and my father talked while I walked over to Warvold and took his dry and bony hand in mine. He drew me near his weathered face, his eyes still the bright green of a young man, and he whispered in my ear: "Later, when the sun is low and things have gone quiet, meet me in the dining room and we will take a walk down the streets of Bridewell."

With the greetings complete and work to be done, it was time for me to go, off to set up my room. On my way up the creaking oak stairs, my one bag in hand, I looked back at the massive smoking room; stone walls, dust dancing in the air, the echo of important men becoming reacquainted. I felt much too young to care about the politics of running our towns, and I sensed a strange sensation as my father glanced my way. His look told me I was not welcome in these discussions, because it was not safe for me to know what they would speak of. Lurking in dark corners and listening to what I might hear would be met with unpleasant results.

As long as I could remember, we always stayed in the

same rooms, and no one else ever came with us or was a guest while we were visiting. Warvold had but one child, a son, who managed the affairs of Lunenburg in his absence. I too was an only child, and though I loved my mother, the annual trips to Bridewell were for my father and me alone. Warvold's wife had passed away only two years after the wall was completed, and he had not remarried (her name was Renny, thus the naming of the lodge). Ganesh remained restless and enjoyed the freedom of solitary life, and so always arrived alone and seemed perfectly content to do so.

Along the third floor hallway, the smell was musty and dry, a smell I acquainted with adventure and freedom. A few steps beyond the stairwell were the doors to my favorite place in Renny Lodge: the library. There were many wonderful books in Bridewell Common, and most of them were kept at Renny Lodge, guarded by my best friend in Bridewell, an old codger named Grayson. The library was closed at this hour, so I turned in the opposite direction and walked to my room near the other end of the hall. I could hear distant voices traveling the stairs, rising into a meaningless garble.

My room looked out over a sea of bright green ivy climbing up and over the wall. I gazed out along the edge where the rock became entwined with distant colors. I would be in Bridewell for the next thirty days with almost no supervision. While my father was busy running the kingdom, I would be busy exploring. And maybe, just maybe—this summer I would find what I had been looking for every other summer that I had come here.

A way outside the wall.

PERVIS KOTCHER

From my room, and as far as I know my room *only*, a person could catch a glimpse of the world outside of Bridewell. If I stood on the sill of my window, which was about three feet off the floor, I could look out from the top edge of the opening. From this vantage point I could see over the wall and into the distance. When I arrived in my room I stood in the sill and looked out as far as I could in every direction.

I hopped down and went to my bag, unfastened the strap, and flipped open the leather cover. My father had scolded me for not packing more warm clothes, but the truth was I needed the extra room in my bag for other things.

Once all my clothing was put away, I went to work untying the lace in the center of what appeared to be the bottom of the bag. I had sewn in two extra leather flaps, which met in the middle and were tightly tied together. This created the illusion of a bottom, and covered the lower third of the space in my bag. I flopped the covers back, uncovering a curious collection of objects.

Hard candy from home, a pouch of coins, and a book; a wallet with small metal tools purchased from a traveling merchant in Lathbury; a compass, stationary with pen and ink, my letter seal, candles and wood matches, an old watch. I rifled through my collection and found the item I was searching for:

26

a small, ornate spyglass, an item that I had borrowed without asking from one of the drawers in my mother's bedroom.

I slid the cylindrical overlapping sections open and ran my hand over the smooth, decorated surface. Paisley patterns of orange and purple flowed watery along its face, with smart brass rings at the butt of each section. I clawed my way back onto the sill and peered through the spyglass. I could see rolling hills in the distance, mostly treeless and covered with thick brush in different shades of green.

To the right, just in view, was the Turlock gate and its twin guard towers. This was where the one person in Bridewell who despised me spent a good bit of his time, a wretched little man who was convinced that everything outside the wall was evil and dangerous. For reasons I have never understood, Warvold loved him, and had even made him captain of the guards. I had to concede, his tenacity for patrolling the streets and walls of Bridewell was legendary, but his suspicious demeanor weighed heavily against him. He seemed to naturally sense my interest in the world outside, and on every visit I had made in the past, he shadowed me relentlessly. Mean, nasty, and always watching me, to my thinking, that summed up Pervis Kotcher.

My eye caught a tick of movement and I was distracted from my thoughts of Pervis. Outside the northeast wall, the valley floor quickly turned to rolling hills, each one growing steadily higher and higher until they disappeared in the mist. The brush was thick and gnarly, colored in greens, browns, and reds. The further the hills, the more the brush created a tapestry of color, ever darker. In the distance, they took on a somber, uninviting appearance.

I saw the movement again, about a hundred yards from the edge of the wall in a patch of red. Could it be a large animal roaming in The Dark Hills, or an evil beast stirring in the dense thicket? I drew the spyglass to my eye, squinting into the lens as I panned the spyglass back and forth. Except for a rustle from the prevailing wind, the brush was still. Maybe all I had seen was a bush shaken in the breeze.

I continued inspecting the area, but eventually my neck burned and my back grew sore enough that I took a break. I collapsed my spyglass and turned to jump down off the sill, and there he was, standing in front of me.

"Well, well, well. Alexa Daley." I yelped, lost my balance, and came tumbling out of the sill. It was Pervis Kotcher.

"What am I to do with you, Alexa?" he said, a condescending grin smeared across his thin lips. I rubbed my knee with one hand and placed the spyglass in my back pocket with the other. I hoped he hadn't seen me using it. I rose and looked at him, feeling even smaller than my four and a half foot frame.

Pervis was barely a foot taller than I was. He wore his black hair at shoulder length and he had deep-set dark eyes. One can become lost in the depths of certain dark eyes, especially those of the handsome or pretty. But Pervis had eyes that reminded me more of rats and other creatures of the night, and I was forever turning away when I encountered them staring back at me.

He held his finger to his mouth, elbow in hand, tapping on his thin lips as he stared at me. He had added a wimpy mustache during my absence.

"I see you're back, and as careless as ever." He paced around my room until he neared my open bag. "It's been a nice summer so far in Bridewell, hardly a reason to work if you're a man of the uniform these days—just one lazy day after another. But of course, now that you're back, I'll have plenty to keep me busy, now won't I?" He hovered over my bag, ready to reach inside and dig through its contents.

"I think the mustache makes you look shorter," I said, knowing I was taking a risk in a room alone with him. He jerked his hand back from my bag and pointed it at me.

"Let's get one thing clear right now," he said. "If I see you on the sill again, I'll have a chat with your father." He paused, glared at me, and placed his hand upon the black stick hanging at his side. "I'm watching you, Alexa Daley. So much as go *near* the wall, and you'll find my club against your knees—do we understand each other?"

I nodded yes.

"Oh, and one more thing—I'll take that spyglass in your back pocket," said Pervis. "I wouldn't want any crazy ideas getting into your head."

"I don't know what you're talking about."

Pervis raised his voice. "Give me the spyglass *now*, or I'll march you downstairs and make you give it to me in front of your father, Ganesh, and Warvold."

If my father found out I'd been spying outside the wall, let alone with a telescope I'd stolen from my mother, it would seriously restrict my freedom for the duration of the trip. I pulled it out of my pocket, had a last good look at it, and tossed it to him.

"You're a nobody, Alexa. A worm. And just between you and me, so is your father." He started back for my bag, about to put his hand in, a surly grin on his face, when footsteps approached my room. Pervis quickly concealed my spyglass in his jacket and ran his hands through his stringy hair.

Into the doorway strode Warvold, looking curiously at Pervis. "Kotcher, what are you doing here?" he said, standing his ground between my room and the hallway.

"Just catching up on old times with Alexa. We haven't seen each other for some time you know," said Pervis.

Warvold stared at him accusingly, then moved out of the doorway.

"Back to work with you, protecting the city from evil hordes and all that. Alexa and I have a date for which you have already made us late," said Warvold.

Pervis glanced my way. I could tell he was thinking about

29

revealing the spyglass, but he didn't.

"Very well, sir, as you wish," said Pervis. He bowed and slithered out the door.

Warvold escorted me out of my room, down the stairs, and out into the night. The walk ended in his death, as I explained at the beginning of this story, and it left me all alone, far away from the lodge, too scared to move.

After he died, I huddled up against the wall, searching for what little warmth remained locked away in the giant stones. My eyes fell upon the locket around Warvold's lifeless neck, and then to his closed fist clutching the locket key, which got me to thinking about things one really should not be thinking about at a time like this. If ever there were a person who would know how to get outside the wall, it would have been Warvold. I didn't know what other things the key might unlock, but I had a suspicion that possessing it might get me one step closer to sitting with my back against the other side of the wall.

My desire for the gate key gave me an ounce of courage, just enough courage it turns out to touch the cold bony wrist of a dead man in the dark.

Without his coat on, old Warvold's wrist was thin and bare, cold and clammy, covered with a dry dust of desert skin. Wrapping my hand around his bare wrist, I lifted his heavy and lifeless arm. At that moment all of the shock I had been feeling left me, and I realized for the first time that my old friend Warvold was really gone. I'd never talk to him again, or hold his hand in mine, or listen to one of his gothic stories. I expected to feel dread when I touched his spiritless skin; instead I was sad and lonely. I sat in the dark, held Warvold's comforting hand, and cried bitterly.

It took me a long time to gain my composure, but finally I began to lift Warvolds hand up so I could pry the key out of his clinched fist. About half way up I lost my grip and dropped his arm into the dirt with a thud. I carefully turned his arm over and set it in his lap, peeled his fingers open like a banana, and revealed the golden key. I drew the key up and unlatched the locket, then put the key back in Warvold's hand and closed his dead fingers around it. Inside the locket I found two more keys.

I held the locket with one hand and removed the keys: one large and gold, the other small and silver. After thinking it over I returned the large one, the one that had opened the gate, thinking it best that something reside inside the locket to avoid suspicion when my father or Ganesh eventually checked it. My fear and sadness turned the corner into exhilaration as I pocketed the small silver key.

I rose to my feet, surprisingly sore from sitting in the cold so long. After a final glance back at Warvold, I began walking in the direction of Renny Lodge.

THE LIBRARY

Upon my return to Renny Lodge with the news of Warvold's death, I met Ganesh in the smoking room enjoying a pipe by the fire. He held me tight, warming both my body and my downcast spirit, and we sat quietly for several minutes with hardly a word spoken between us. When my father arrived he was immediately more practical about the matter.

"Where is the body? Are you all right, Alexa? We should think about what ought to be done next." But even my father, with his pragmatic approach to things, had eventually flopped down next to me on the couch, his head in his hands.

It fell now on Ganesh and my father to get things right, become the elder statesmen, and take care of us all. As they sat in the flickering glow of the fireplace that night, the sense of responsibility they both faced weighed on them, forever sealing off a simpler past.

People began streaming back into Bridewell the next day. Within a few hours, hundreds of people had arrived, and once word spread to all the towns a steady flow of humanity rushed in from all directions. By the morning of the funeral, three days after Warvold's death, Bridewell was bursting at the seams. The town was only a few square miles in size, and the guards had let in as many people as it would hold. The rest were lined up in caravans on the roads from Lathbury, Turlock, and Lunenburg.

My father had been in one of the guard towers overlooking the Lunenburg gate, and he told me the line of carts and horses went back for miles.

It was decided that a processional would be the only way to accommodate the large crowds. Throughout the day of the funeral, the guards opened one of the gates and let a dozen carts in on one side and out on the other, then closed the gate and opened the next one a few minutes later. The circular procession lasted until darkness fell on Bridewell.

At the funeral, my father and Ganesh both spoke about Warvold and his many achievements. Listening, I was taken back again by all that he had been: adventurer, architectural genius, devoted leader.

Pervis was as pesky as ever, poking his nose in at every turn, accusing anyone he could of wrong doing, asking pointed questions. He was as surly as I could recall him ever being. The crowds were also a problem, and poor little Bridewell took quite a beating during the days after Warvold's death.

Then, mercifully, things quieted down. Emotions settled and people thinned out. My father and Ganesh got down to the business of planning, and welcomed Nicolas, Warvold's son. Nicolas had the characteristic Warvold drive and ambition, but a generation removed; he was mellow and willing to listen and learn. It was clear that the three of them would work well together, and I thought I might see little of my father for the next few weeks as they met and discussed important issues.

It was time to refocus on the business at hand, which for me meant finding a way outside the wall. Now more than ever I burned to feel the freedom of the forest and the mountains, and I had a new key that I hoped would help me in the process.

At three o'clock on the day after the funeral, with Bridewell reduced to a low hum of remaining visitors and residents, I crept up to the library to visit Grayson and get away from what was left of the crowds. In all the commotion since my arrival

I had not once enjoyed the zigzag isles of books, or heard the intimate creaking along the wooden floors as I browsed lazily for new reading material. Opening the door to the library, I smelled a delightful, familiar odor of old books, and I felt the peaceful quiet this place always emitted.

The library was a maze of high shelves piled ominously toward the ceiling with old volumes. Warvold had been a scholarly traveler, and the library was assembled from books he collected on his many trips. Later, as Warvold's trips became infrequent, he insisted that dignitaries from all the towns in the Land of Elyon requesting a meeting bring a beloved book. The more fascinating or well-crafted volumes garnered a better reception for the caller. As such, the library became widely known as the most expansive and envied in all of Elyon.

Thousands of books on all sorts of subjects lined the passageways. The labyrinth of shelves led off in several directions, some ending at stonewalls, others at wood benches, still more wound around in circles or met up with other rows. But one trail of bookshelves led to what I considered to be the most perfect reading spot in all the world. Around one corner and then another, at the end of a long row, was a nook. In this nook was a small window that overlooked the ivy covered Dark Hills wall. Set back in the corner was a cushy old beat up rag of a chair and a wood box for a footstool. Tranquil, private, cozy. It was heaven on earth.

I often sat in the chair idly reading entire days away, alternately napping and flipping through volume after volume. Many were quite boring actually, legal works and treaties. But others were histories of the cities and towns and regions of our land. The best of the books contained made up stories and legends, and some spoke of exotic animals found in fanciful jungles and marshland. I constantly searched for information about what might be outside the walls in the forest, the mountains, and The Dark Hills. But in all my searching I found almost nothing. A few scant references to the mysterious nature of the magic that prowled around in faraway places sounded like the tales I'd overheard people tell about our own wild area. But there was never much to go on, and never anything about matters close to home, or about what sorts of creatures might slink around outside these walls.

My napping was encouraged by Sam and Pepper, the two library cats that liked to take turns sitting on my lap in the afternoon sun, purring and begging for scratches under their necks. They wore peculiar but beautiful collars, jeweled leather all the way around, and both dangling a small handcrafted medallion. The cats had belonged to the late Renny Warvold, and they had lived in the library for as long as I could remember. They were quite old; I think maybe fifteen or sixteen, and they slept all the time.

Grayson came in five days a week and organized the shelves. He was also a master at repairing old books, and he spent most of his time in a small office in the library, which was used to work on misbehaving spines and torn pages. I loved Grayson even more than I loved the old books. He was kind, gentle, and maybe the best listener I'd ever met.

I walked along the rows of books and poked my head around the corner into Grayson's office. He was hunkered down over a large manuscript which had been removed from its housing, and he was busy devising a new cover to replace the tattered remains of the old leather facing. When he saw me poke my head around the corner into his office, he grinned from ear to ear and stood up to greet me with open arms. His big belly arched my back as we hugged, and I sobbed a little, still tender from all the recent events. I managed to gain my composure and look into his deep brown eyes.

"You've gotten more reclusive since my last visit," I said, pulling up my shirt to dry my face. "How could you miss the largest funeral this place has ever seen?"

Grayson shuffled his feet back and forth nervously. "I know, I know, I should have attended. I hate crowds though, *hate* 'em. I sat up here and pulled out Warvold's favorite books, shined 'em up, unfolded the dog ears, fixed a few ruffled edges." He moved back around to the other side of his desk, running his fingers through a thick gray mustache. When he was seated he picked up a small, tattered book. "See this one? This was Warvold's all time favorite, the one he really loved." He held it out to me and I took it in my hands.

It was medium sized, black, leather bound, and in poor condition. The cover read *Myths and Legends In The Land of Elyon*. Grayson continued, "Warvold loved this stuff. Crazy made up stories and fables from every corner of the land. He would wander in here after a long day of meeting with your father and Ganesh and sit a spell with that book. He'd sit right there, across from me. I would work on books and he would read. It was nice, calm. Then he'd put the book back on the shelf and meander out the door, off to bed or to smoke a pipe by the fireplace."

I flipped through the worn pages: small text, some writing in the margins here and there. "It's sort of beat up. Are you neglecting your duties?"

He smiled. "No Ma'am. The old man never would let me work on that one. He seemed to like it well worn. I guess leaving that shabby old thing alone is my way of honoring him. Believe me; I'd love to make it perfect again: new cover, fix up the pages, clean it all up. But I get the feeling wherever he is, he would rather I left it tattered and torn."

"Can I borrow it for a little afternoon reading?" I said, running my fingers along its cover.

"Sure you can, but take these ones too." He turned to his desk and picked up a stack of books. "These are on topics you were searching for last year: bears, forests, history of surrounding regions, that sort of thing. Not much really, but I've been holding them up here for a while now, so either put them back or get to reading them."

It was so nice to be back in the company of a weathered friend, someone who knew I just needed to sit in my favorite chair and fall asleep reading. Knowing Grayson was in the library with me lent a special peace to the feelings I had about this place. We talked little, but we understood the language of our movements and the need for quiet companionship. I took my books with a wink and made my way down a twisting row of towering books.

Rounding the corner to my chair, I saw a peculiar sight; Sam and Pepper perched on the sill of the small window, and a hawk standing right there with them. When I came into view, the hawk beat its wings furiously, banging them against the stone wall before escaping into the open air. I jumped back, threw my books in all directions, and let out a loud shriek. Warvold's favorite book came apart at the stitching and pages scattered on the floor around me. I stacked the other books on the floorboards next to my chair while I scolded the cats. Both were already on the chair rolled over on their sides waiting for me to pet them.

I spent the next ten minutes picking up pages and sorting them out, trying to put the book back into one piece. It was in reasonably good shape when I was done, but it would need some repair work if it were to stay together. Warvold's one and only favorite book had been in my possession for only a few minutes, and already I'd managed to destroy it.

Exasperated, I pushed the cats aside and flopped down in the chair. They crawled up on my lap, and shortly thereafter I fell into a deep sleep.

More Trouble with My Spyglass

I awoke slowly in the late afternoon heat, sweaty and sticky after what must have been an hour's nap. I felt around for the cats but they were gone, which was odd, because when I slept in the library they always stayed with me. After I rubbed the sleep out of my eyes and opened them I saw why they had moved on.

"I was wondering when you might wake up." It was Pervis Kotcher. He was close enough that I could smell his breath, rank from a recent cup of strong coffee. He moved to the window, drew my mother's beautiful spyglass to his eye, and mockingly looked about the wall.

"What do you want?" I asked. Even in my sleepy state I was surprisingly irritated.

"I was just doing my rounds and I thought I might spy something with my new spyglass," he said. "The thing is, it isn't a very good one. I've half a mind to throw it out." He collapsed the spyglass and placed it in the pocket of his uniform, then turned towards me, an evil squint on his nauseating face.

"I saw you and Warvold when you went out by the wall. I lost sight of you from my tower, but you were out there a long time. Then I saw you slink past the gate, no big rush, just tottering back to Renny Lodge."

He had a hand on each arm of my chair, locking me into

my seat, leaning his face close to mine. I was uncomfortable and scared and I wished badly that he would go away.

"Now, Alexa," he said, a foul wave of his breath washing over my face, "what am I to think? Gone for over an hour with Warvold in a place you shouldn't be, carelessly skipping back to the lodge, and right after that we find him dead." Then Pervis said something strange.

"Has anyone contacted you from outside the wall?"

"Who's outside?"

"Don't lie to me, Alexa!" He yelled. He was visibly upset.

"What's all the fuss back there?" It was Grayson coming up the aisle, the floorboards creaking as he came.

"Nothing. Nothing at all," said Pervis. "Go back to your books." Grayson stayed right where he was, but I knew bravery was not one of his strongest characteristics.

"I said go back to your books," said Pervis, one hand on his guard stick. Grayson shuffled backwards, turned, and walked away. Pervis looked back at me with a prideful sneer. He let the uncomfortable still moment hang in the air as the sound of Grayson's footsteps got farther and farther away. He paced back to the window and leaned forward into the sill with his hands clasped behind his back, looking for a long moment at the green and gray of the wall.

"You know Alexa, now that Warvold is gone, I can do whatever I want. Your father and Ganesh can't control me. No one can," he said.

"How can you talk like that?" I pleaded.

"I open my mouth and words come out, what could be easier?"

His thoughtless reply upset me. "My father and Ganesh are in charge now, *not* you—"

"I answer to *no* one, least of all your worthless father!" Pervis shot back, loud and unthinking, and right then Grayson rounded the corner with Ganesh in tow.

Pervis went a deep red, stammered, and backed up against the window.

Ganesh had one of the cats in hand, scratching its head playfully. "I love these cats don't you, Kotcher? So calm and gentle." Confrontation was not in Grayson's vocabulary, and he was well on his way back to his office by the time Ganesh set the cat down. "Off you go now, catch some mice."

Ganesh looked squarely down at Pervis, towering over his short, squat frame. Pervis tried to speak, but Ganesh put his hand up and motioned him to stop. "I want to make sure I have all the facts straight. I'd hate to misrepresent you, now that I understand the magnitude of your power."

Pervis turned redder, his lips thinned, a scowl flashed across his face.

"I think what I heard was, 'I answer to Ganesh and Nicolas, but most of all, I answer to Mr. Daley' is that correct, or did I leave something out?" said Ganesh. I couldn't help grinning, and Pervis shot me a wicked glance.

"It was either that," said Ganesh, "or maybe it was that other thing I thought you might have said, which will drop your rank to private in charge of cleaning horse stalls and peeling potatoes. Which do you remember?"

Pervis was ready to give in, ready to concede defeat. He was a hothead, but he was also smart. He looked at me, then at Ganesh, then he reached into his pocket and pulled out the spyglass. He smiled.

"I apologize," he said. "Alexa has given me some trouble in the past and she's up to something now, that much I know. I got a little carried away. Of course you three are in charge, absolutely. I won't let it happen again, sir."

He gestured to the spyglass and went on, "Anyway, this toy belongs to Alexa, I found it lying around the smoking room." Then pointing at me, speaking like a parent to a small child, he continued. "You really should take better care of your things,

Alexa. Next time I find it I'll throw it away." And with that, he held the spyglass out to me. I was so excited to have it back I reached out to grab it. Pervis pulled it back, turned its face to the side, and slammed it into the wall with all his might, smashing all of the glass out of the cylinder.

"No!" I cried.

"Now Ganesh, you know a spyglass is strictly forbidden in Bridewell, unless of course you're a member of the guard, like me. Poor Alexa here will have to do without the glass I'm afraid. Sorry, but rules are rules, and they must be followed." Said Pervis. "Here you go dear, you can have it now."

I took the broken spyglass in my hand and began to cry. Ganesh looked like he was ready to throw Pervis through the window, but what could he do? I shouldn't have brought the thing to Bridewell in the first place.

Ganesh told Pervis to get out, and he was happy to do just that, but not before he made sure I got his 'I told you not to mess with me' look. I found out later he stopped to talk with Grayson on the way out. He told him how snitches have their beds loaded with vermin at night; just the kind of veiled threat Pervis enjoyed using.

I pocketed the broken spyglass and dried my tears. It was turning out to be a bad week indeed. Ganesh held out his hand and I took it. Warm, big, safe. He lifted me out of the chair and up into a hug, then he spoke with his wonderful, deep voice. "I'll get Kotcher off your back so you can explore Bridewell a little more freely. I know how you love to go sneaking around, and I'm all for it as long as nobody gets hurt." He started tickling me, first with his beard, then with his free hand at my belly. I writhed loose and tumbled down into the chair, feeling much better. We both smiled.

"The problem we have with Kotcher is that he ' around a long time," said Ganesh. "And he is v protecting Bridewell. His guards are always in to works tirelessly, and his reports are excellent. He's just para-noid about the outside, and you seem to bring out the worst in him, which is bad indeed." He said. "To be honest Alexa, I'm not sure how safe I'd feel if he wasn't around. Sometimes you have to take the good with the bad to get what you need. It's something your dad and I are still figuring out."

Then he tickled me again until Grayson could be heard coming down the corridor of books. "What's all the fuss back there?"

My week was getting better, but it was about to get down-right spectacular.

JOCASTAS

Following my afternoon nap I was feeling energized. I joined my father, Ganesh, and Nicolas for dinner off the smoking room in the main dining area. It was good to spend time with them, especially my father, who was looking a little worn out.

"I'd ask you to pass the bread, but you look so beat I'm not sure you could get it all the way over here," I said.

"You should join the jesters class in session downstairs, I hear they're looking for a good teacher," said my father. He did look tired, and even his comeback came off weak as he tried to bring some mental energy to the conversation.

"That's all right, Daley, you keep trying. Determination is one of your best qualities," said Ganesh.

"A distant third to my charm and good looks," added my father.

We talked and ate for over an hour, enjoying the easy quality of our evening meal. It was the most free-spirited gathering of the day and we all looked forward to it. Nicolas was captivating, and he really did fit right in with all of us. He shared funny stories about Warvold and we all laughed, and he knew when to let someone else have a chance to talk after he'd been going for a while. He was a good-looking fellow, tall, with dark trimmed hair and no beard or mustache.

"Did I tell you I promoted our new friend Silas Hardy?"

asked my father.

"Who?" I replied.

"That nice delivery man we raced on the way to Bridewell. I've made him our private courier, which means he carries letters for me whenever I want, and burns all of the ones Ganesh tries to send out. Hardy and I are committed to saving poor Ganesh from embarrassing himself."

"Daley, you've got tongue enough for ten rows of teeth," said Ganesh.

"And you're so ugly your mother had to slap herself when you were born," said my father. This went on for some time, the details of which are not worthy of repeating here.

I wanted to get the conversation back over to Nicolas so after a while I interrupted with a question. "Nicolas, can you tell me about your mother, Renny? I know almost nothing about her and I'd like to learn more."

Ganesh and my father settled down and reloaded their plates while Nicolas drank his wine and gathered his thoughts.

"Let's see, my mother was tall and slender and pretty, with dark hair and good teeth. I always remember her good teeth, I'm not sure why. Funny how our memories work, isn't it? Holding onto the strangest details about a person." He paused to take another sip of wine, and Ganesh kindly refilled the glass.

Nicolas gestured his thanks and went on. "She was terribly interested in precious stones and jewels. My father had quite a collection of rare gems from his travels. Some he traded for, others he won gambling. I'm told he was quite a hotshot at cards and dice, and I suspect he crisscrossed the globe taking advantage of rich young rulers wherever he went.

"Renny began making her own bracelets and rings, just trinkets really, but she was good at it. I think most considered her a craftswoman of a high order. Later she became interested in tiny detailed etchings on sapphires and rubies called Jocastas, and the art remained her passion until she died." Nicolas pulled a necklace from beneath his shirt with a large stone attached.

He held it out so we could see it clearly. "You can't see the real detail, because it's covered by a pattern which hides the real essence of the piece. On the surface you see an elaborate etching, but if you had a powerful magnifying glass, you'd see that the Jocasta within is a rendering of our family seal: a crown of thorns." Nicolas showed the stone to each of us up close, and then turned it on himself, straining to see the details below the surface.

"I was in such a rush to get here I left my glass in Lunenburg, otherwise I would show it to you. I don't know how many she did, maybe thirty. The locket my father wore has a similar looking pattern, only the Jocasta is two tiny hearts with an arrow through them, symbolic of the bond between my mother and father."

I found the idea of the Jocasta fascinating and wondered aloud if Nicolas knew of any more she had done that were still in existence.

"They took an awful long time to make, sometimes months for just one, so there weren't many to begin with. For all I know she only made a few instead of a few dozen. She gave them as gifts to close relatives and friends. My aunt has one, and there are a few in with the family jewels, but that's all I know of.

"In any case, without a powerful magnifying glass, you wouldn't know a Jocasta gem if it was sitting in your hand." Nicolas drank again from his wine. I seem to recall good wine as something Warvold enjoyed. It was clear his son was fond of it as well. "When I return home I'll bring my glass so we can look at this one," and he held out his necklace again. "Or I suppose we could send Silas off to get it, since there are only letters from Ganesh to deliver this week."

The three of them were quickly back at it again. I wondered how long it would take for my father and Ganesh to begin calling Nicolas by his last name, or if they ever would. It seemed that with them, you were a Daley, a Ganesh, a Warvold or Kotcher. Being called by your last name indicated you were an important adult to these men. I doubted they would ever call me anything but Alexa.

As they continued into the evening, wine flowing as freely as well-timed insults, I slinked out and went to my bedroom. I had seen my mother during the funeral, but she had only stayed for a day. My mother, much like Grayson and me, hated crowds, and this was the biggest crowd in the smallest space she or I had ever encountered. The walls had made it seem as though we were millions of ants locked in a glass jar, stepping over and crawling under each other.

I had to send her a letter, a letter I really did not look forward to writing, but longed to be finished with. I dressed for bed and tidied up my room, flitting about in an effort to avoid my desk. I even reclined on my bed and started reading Warvold's book, which I had snuck out of the library, hoping I might tire out and fall asleep. But my guilt overwhelmed me. Sitting at my desk with pen in hand, I thus began:

Dear mother,

I do hope your trip home was not too long. I suspect you encountered more dust than either of us knew could be kicked up by carts from here to Lathbury. I'm sure you endured a long day of travel, but it feels good to know you are home safe and sound.

Things have settled down here, almost back to nor-mal. I enjoyed dinner with father and Ganesh and Nicolas this evening. Everyone seems taken with Nicolas and I think he will do just fine. Father is tired, working too hard again—but we are getting along well, and we find our spare moments to wander off together often enough for the both of us.

I must tell you something now that I hope you will not punish me too greatly for upon my return home, though I will deserve nothing less than a sound thrashing with a willow. I wanted desperately to see farther outside the wall on my visit than I have been able to in the past, and so I took your spyglass from your drawer and brought it with me. It gets worse. Pervis Kotcher saw me using it, and he took it from me. Later, he returned it, but not before smashing the glass out.

I am sorry mother. I promise to work day and night until I earn enough to repair this precious item that belongs to you. I know I was wrong to take it without asking. Can you forgive me?

I'm off to bed now, lots to do tomorrow. Grayson says hi.

My love,
Alexa

I folded the letter, addressed it to my mother, then dripped wax on it from my candle and applied my seal. I would give it to Silas at breakfast.

I went back to my bed and began flipping through Warvold's old book. I began to feel sleepy almost immediately, and placed the book under my pillow, paranoid that Pervis would be lurking around my room in the middle of the night looking through my things. Which reminded me, what did he mean when he had said "has someone contacted you from outside the wall?" It was an odd thing to say, and I rolled it over in my mind for several minutes until I drifted off to sleep.

THE FIRST JOCASTA

The next day Bridewell was still noisy with the last of the visitors streaming out of the gates toward home. As I walked around, I saw Pervis and his men raising and lowering different gates, checking identifications, searching carts, and generally controlling the flow of people out of Bridewell. I had to admit, he ran a tight ship, and his men seemed more than agreeable to follow his lead.

During my morning stroll around town, I noticed Silas waiting his turn at the Lathbury gate, and I ran to his cart to greet him. I had given Silas my letter at breakfast, and he had been more than happy to get on the road and deliver it personally to my mother's front gate. "You're father has a package for her as well. She will be so pleased to hear from you both," he had said. If only he knew how unhappy my mother was sure to be after reading my letter.

I arrived at the side of his cart and looked up at him. "It looks as though you have a bit of a wait getting out of town. Six carts in front of yours and the sun is already baking the leather off your boots."

"I'm a traveling man Alexa, always have been. Being on my cart with Maiden and Jaz pulling me around is fine by me, no matter the weather," said Silas.

"Try not to get those old sawhorses into any races on the

way home. They might go belly up this time and leave you stranded," I said.

"Stop making fun of my horses!" yelled Silas. He was right; it was a careless attempt at being witty. A bad habit I had picked up from my father.

"Sorry, Silas," I moved in front of Maiden and Jaz and patted their noses softly. "And sorry to you too. You are grand steeds, head and shoulders above all the other horses in the Bridewell barn." This put a smile on Silas's face, and he gave me a wink. I liked Silas; he was my kind of mail carrier.

The gate opened and carts lurched forward. I jumped out of the way so the horses could advance, and they stumbled forward a few steps, now five carts from being set free on the road to Lathbury. Silas had some waiting left to do, and I decided to head back to the library before my reading spot became so hot I would sooner fry an egg on my chair than sit on it.

Upon arrival, I went to see Grayson, but he was strangely absent. His office was in its normal state: half repaired books piled up all over, various tools strewn about, a sweater half hanging, half falling off a chair. He had been in, that much was for sure, since it was he who opened the library every morning. He must have stepped into the kitchen for something to eat.

I shrugged my shoulders and walked in the direction of my chair, stopping on the way to retrieve a volume of stories and a favorite book of poetry. I also had Warvold's book with me, which I planned to spend the better part of the morning browsing through.

Safely tucked into my chair, I had a brief moment of anxiety as I realized the possibility of another encounter with Pervis, only this time Grayson was not in the library to save me. Just as I was nursing this unpleasant thought, Sam jumped up on my lap, followed a second later by Pepper. They purred and dug their heads into my chest looking for all the scratching they could get. I kept rubbing Pepper's belly, only to have him turn and force his head under my hand.

"Since when did you cast off belly rubs?" I said out loud. He just kept on pushing his head into my chest, and then Sam started in with the same routine. I grabbed them both by the nape and lifted them up to my face. I stared them in the eye and they each gave a single "Meow". Then my gaze focused down to the jeweled collars and the medallions hanging from them.

For a moment I went cold, then I started hyperventilating with quick, short breaths, like I did when I realized Warvold was dead. "Meow, Meow!" the cats screamed. I had forgotten I was still holding them both up by the back of the neck on two feet each.

I set them both down and apologized as I tried to gain my composure. The cats sat at attention and I took their collars in my hands. The medallions were each about an inch square; one was green and one red. They were adorned with beautiful alternating patterns. Since the cats had belonged to Renny, it was certainly possible that the medallions contained Jocastas. I was beside myself with anticipation about what they might reveal, and I knew exactly where I could find what I needed to unlock the mystery of the gems.

I leapt up, quickly placing the cats on the chair and pointing my finger at them, "Don't go anywhere you two. I'll be right back." I ran down the zigzag aisles of books towards the front of the library.

When I arrived at the door to Grayson's office, I was overjoyed to find that he had yet to return from what I could only assume was a raid on the kitchen baked goods and a cup of tea. I crept into his office and slid open the drawers to his desk. Grayson was more of a slob than I had imagined, and the first two drawers were completely jammed with wads of paper, spines from old books, and various tools in ill repair. One drawer after another turned up the same collection of junk. The last drawer

I looked in contained a half eaten sandwich ripe from at least a week of neglect. It smelled worse than PKB (my new favorite acronym, which stood for Pervis Kotcher Breath).

I slumped back in Grayson's chair and scanned the shelves, also loaded with old books and other junk. At the end of one shelf was a wood box with a latch. The box had been neglected for some time and the lid was covered with dust. Upon opening it, I found a number of old tools, and the one thing I had been looking for: a printer's glass ring. It was just the thing for viewing a Jocasta. Powerful and precise, the printer's ring was used to magnify broken type and aide in the meticulous filling in of old letters on a printed page. Grayson had long since given up the practice in favor of making the books look good on the outside. "Good riddance to fixing type," he had told me several summers ago, "nobody cares and it's making me old."

I closed the box and I was just about to place it back on the shelf when I heard the library door open. Footsteps approached as I fumbled with the box, and I almost dropped it to the floor with a bang before safely replacing it where I had found it. I pocketed the printer's glass ring just as Grayson appeared in the doorway.

He grinned, rubbing his belly. A red, sticky looking substance crowned his gray mustache. "I tell you Alexa, that kitchen makes the best fresh strawberry jam anywhere. Mmmm, mmmm, I could eat it on baked rolls all day long." From the looks of Grayson's belly, he had been partaking of the Renny Lodge culinary delights on a frequent basis.

"You better cut back on the kitchen raids Grayson, your walk is turning into a waddle," I said.

"Don't make fun of old people, it's in bad taste." We both smiled as he entered the office.

"What are you doing in here anyway? If you're looking for something to eat, check that bottom right drawer. Fresh vittles from the chef."

Under normal circumstances he would have had me fooled, but since I already knew the drawer contained a most rancid surprise, I passed on his offer and bid my farewell.

"Please be there cats, please be there cats," I repeated as I walked back to my chair. I turned the corner and I saw them sitting at attention, waiting for my return just as I had left them, licking their paws absently.

My hands shook as I removed the tool from my pocket and positioned myself on my knees in front of the cats. Taking Sam's medallion in hand, I placed the printer's glass against its face, and squinted into the device. At first it seemed like nothing more than a jumble of dots and intricate lines. Then, I focused the glass ring by turning it on its dial with a *tic, tic, tic*. The tiny dots and lines came together to form a wave of pathways, but there was no clear beginning or end, and no indication of what their purpose was; just a scattered collection of winding trails. Could it be the streets of Bridewell, or maybe the pathways along the wall? There was a miniature, sparkling mountain at the end of one dotted pathway, but that was the only clear suggestion of a place I could find. Renny really had been talented; this was an amazing piece of hidden artwork.

I raced back to Grayson's office to borrow an ink pen and some paper, returned, and meticulously duplicated the map on a full sheet. My lower back burned with pain from stooping over, and my eye watered from the intense scrutiny of the Jocasta. I could now understand why Grayson had given up the process of fixing broken type.

Finally happy with my depiction of the etching in the Jocasta, I placed it on the sill so the ink could dry. I stood with a creak, my back screaming as I reached for the ceiling to stretch out my crumpled body. I was finished investigating Sam's medallion, so I got back down on my knees and hunched in front of Pepper. As I went to place the gem in my hand, Pepper violently screeched and lashed out with a bared claw, ripping a cruel scratch across the back of my hand. Wincing in pain I scrambled back, lost my grip on the printer's glass, and hurled it as I jerked my hand away.

I heard it hit, and the pain in my hand was nothing compared to the crashing disappointment of hearing the lens pop against the stone wall. Even worse, I heard Grayson running down the aisles of books in my direction, hollering my name over and over in a worried tone. I had only enough time to grab the printer's glass and see that the lens was covered with a spidery crack. I struggled to my feet and pocketed the second item I had both stolen and broken in the span of only a few days.

"What's going on back here?" said Grayson as he rounded the corner. "I haven't heard either of these cats screech like that in years." Then he saw my hand.

"Oh my," said Grayson. "That's a deep one. What did you do, pull his whiskers out?"

I didn't know what to say, so I just stood there, blood oozing down my arm. Then I realized I'd left the map I'd drawn sitting on the window sill, and I moved between it and Grayson, blocking the map from view. "I guess he was just in a bad mood today," I said.

"Let me take a look, make sure you're not going to bleed to death," said Grayson. He took my hand and moved into the light at the windowsill. I stammered a little but couldn't find the right words to stop him. "Calm down," said Grayson, and then he was examining my hand in the warm light, turning it and dabbing it with his handkerchief.

"I think you'll be all right," he said. "It's actually not so bad, only *looks* terrible. Best thing for it is to leave it out in the open so it can scab over. In a few days, you will hardly notice it except for the itching."

Then he let my hand go, gave me a long, solemn look, and said: "I have a hankering for some strawberry jam on biscuits.

How about you join me for a stroll down to the kitchen?"

With a faint smile I nodded yes, and we began to walk toward the front of the library. At least we were away from my drawing. I just hoped nobody would find it while I was gone.

We walked the aisles of books, stopping here and there to fix up a shelf, a habit both Grayson and I had acquired from spending so much time wandering in the library.

"By the way," said Grayson. "That's a mighty nice map of the library you did. Very impressive."

"What did you say?"

"You're drawing on the window sill back there. It must have taken you quite a while to figure out how this place winds around. I think you got close, at least it looked good from what little I saw."

My hand was shaking in Grayson's.

"Are you all right, Alexa? Maybe we should pay a visit to a real doctor and make sure that hand is okay, you're shaking like a leaf."

I looked up at Grayson with a big smile. "No, I'm just so excited to try those biscuits and strawberry jam I can hardly wait." And I began pulling Grayson down the row of books towards the kitchen.

ALONE IN BRIDEWELL

I wasn't ready to go searching around the library when I returned with Grayson, so I retrieved the map and ran to my room. I stayed alone for a while and thought about what I would do next, then I went to the kitchen for dinner. When I returned to my room I sat on my windowsill, folded my arms around my knees, and gazed into the misty orange glow of the sunset. The evening breeze was a welcome change from the smoldering heat of the day. I had Warvold's silver key in one hand, the drawing of the etching in the Jocasta fluttering back and forth in the other. An hour later the orange sunset had turned to black night and I lurched out of the windowsill, crossed the room, and sat down on my bed.

I had a fitful night of sleep wrought with dreams of Pervis Kotcher's head bobbing grotesquely atop a cat's body, the feline-man thing chasing me from room to room around the lodge. In the morning I awoke, dressed, and went to the kitchen. It was already hot, and the light breeze had completely disappeared. The sun would stoke Bridewell like a furnace all morning, and bring it to a staggering boil by midday. I wondered how it might feel beneath the tall trees outside the wall on the cool forest floor.

Breakfast was buzzing more than usual. Grayson showed up for more strawberry preserves, this time on pancakes. Ganesh, my father, and Nicolas were in a debate over land use and expansion between Lunenburg and Ainsworth. Silas had returned from Lathbury earlier in the morning and he was busy putting the finishing touches on a plate filled with toast, biscuits, and hotcakes, all of it covered with thick red jam, no doubt on advice from Grayson.

I poked Silas in the ribs from behind and greeted him, "Back so soon? I thought you would be gone at least another day."

Both he and Grayson turned in my direction. "You know those old horses of mine, they would rather ride in the dark than in the heat of the day," said Silas, and then he looked at me with a squinted eye. "If you tell them I said that, I'll glue your shoes together."

"I see you've discovered the fresh strawberry jam," I said. "Grayson is guzzling it by the gallon. I think he's a bear dressed up like a man, getting an early start on hibernation."

Grayson, a familiar red bead circling his thick mustache, raised one eyebrow at me, and put an entire pancake slathered with jam into his mouth in one bite. It was disgusting.

"Any word from my mother?" I said, hoping the answer was no.

"I waited as long as I could, but she was out when I arrived. I did leave your letter and a note that I would return in a few days if she had anything for you or your father. I'm sure she will send it along."

Relieved, I drifted over to the buffet and filled a plate with food, and then I sat down next to my father. Nicolas was talking, and he was right in the middle of making a point.

"...I tell you, if you don't pay attention to Ainsworth, they will one day rule Bridewell. They are bigger than we are, and we control safe passages through dangerous territory. We must expand Lunenburg northwest towards them before they sprawl too far. I know they seem friendly now, but I don't trust them, and neither did my father."

I received a warm good morning from my father, Ganesh, and Nicolas, and then they continued on, my father with his hand on my shoulder. It felt good to have his arm around me.

This was called fishing. Whenever my father and Ganesh were looking for opinions from everyday folks about issues of the day, they would float the topic out like fish bait and see which point of view caused the hook to be swallowed whole. Obviously, they had initiated Nicolas into this tactic as well, since he had thrown out the first line.

"I could not disagree more," said Ganesh, my father giving me a hidden wink. "If we build towards them they'll see it as hostile and we'll be pulled into a confrontation. Now I agree that we've got to expand, these last few days in Bridewell have clearly shown that. Within a few years Bridewell and the towns against the sea will be at maximum capacity, and then what will we do?

"We have over ten miles between us and Ainsworth, which I think is a good healthy distance. We can't expand off the cliffs from Lathbury or Turlock, so those are dead ends. Bridewell is stuck in the middle with no place to grow. I think our best option is to start building two and three story buildings. Grow up instead of out. We could grow to twice our size if we just abolished the one level rule," said Ganesh.

"That's an extremely bad idea." It was Pervis, who had quietly arrived at the dining room entryway unnoticed. He was leaning against the wall, hands crossed over his chest.

"Why aren't you out protecting us all from the boogieman?" said my father. It gave me the creeps when he said it, but everyone else seemed to think it was funny.

"Laugh all you want, but I'm telling you, building higher is a dangerous idea. It exposes us to the outside and makes us vulnerable," said Pervis. "And once people start spending all their free time looking for strange things outside the wall you'll have an even bigger problem. Get common folks curious, and you might just as well set Bridewell on a barrel of gunpowder."

He was at the buffet now, loading up on eggs. I didn't like where he was taking the conversation.

"Take Alexa for instance," Pervis continued. "We give her the only room in Bridewell that has a window with a teensy view over the wall. She's only a child, and we assume a child is timid and afraid. What interest would a child have in the outside? But even sweet little Alexa here figured out that if she stands in the sill she can get a little taste of what's out there. And *then* what does she do?"

Here it comes; I'm as good as grounded for the rest of my life.

"She brings a spyglass to Bridewell, and parks herself up in that sill looking for who knows what. A *spyglass.* Those things have been banned in Bridewell for as long as I can remember. Or did you all have a change of heart and forget to tell old Pervis about it?"

I wished I'd have skipped breakfast and gone straight to the library. I expected my father to recoil, to take his arm from around my tiny shoulder. He would have had every right. Instead, he gripped my scrawny arm tightly in his big hand and pulled me closer. He reached over with his fork and stole some eggs off my plate, chewing them with deliberate slowness. The room was silent.

"Mr. Kotcher," said my father. "How much longer do you think Ganesh and I will be around?"

I'd seen my father like this before. His tone had changed ever so slightly, but it signified to everyone in the room that his fangs were out.

"I really don't have the faintest idea, sir," said Pervis, staring him down.

My father rose and stood behind me with one hand on each of my shoulders, his firm grip unwavering.

"Take a close look at this girl. She's becoming a young lady, and in a few summers, she'll be a young woman. The day is coming soon when she will be part of the ruling council. She will have her opinions heard; she will be listened to. Unless Ganesh gets with it and has some children soon, Alexa will be running this place with Nicolas before long. She won't need me to come to her defense, and it will be her choice what rank you enjoy, or whether you remain here at all. You would do well to consider these things before opening up your mouth in a crowded room again."

My father sat back down and began eating from his plate. "Will there be anything else, Mr. Kotcher?"

I think Pervis and I both understood for the first time in our lives that one day I would have authority over him. He wasted no time in trying to defend himself. "But *that girl* is a trouble maker. Mark my words Daley, she'll put us in a dangerous situation and she'll bring us all down. I don't know how or when, but she *will* endanger us." He scanned the room for support, but everyone was either looking down at their food or glaring back at him.

"I will not bother her again, but not because I care about the absurdity of a future with her in charge. If I'm not here to run the guards this place will be *totally* vulnerable. I've taken an oath to protect Bridewell, and putting my tail between my legs to suit your ego and your spoiled child is fine by me. So long as Bridewell is safe, that's all I care about." He turned on his heels and stormed out of the room.

Grayson was halfway to the library before Pervis was even out of the dining area. The rest of the group started talking again and milling around. "Would you all mind if Alexa and I excused ourselves?" My father said, and he took me by the hand and walked with me, out of the room, down the stairs, and out the door. We walked for a long time and neither of us said a thing.

Eventually the silence took its toll on me and I gave in with a shower of words.

"I already wrote to mother and told her I took the spyglass, but she hasn't responded. I know I shouldn't have taken it. I'm sorry, I'm so sorry. I just wanted a glimpse of what might be out there." My father was down on one knee shaking me by the shoulders and telling me to stop.

"Calm down, Alexa," he said. He took my hand again, stood up, and we walked to the center of town and sat on a bench.

"Warvold is gone, Alexa. I don't think anyone realizes how significant that is. Me, Ganesh, Nicolas, we're good leaders, but we're not Warvold. He built this place, and he had his own secret reasons for doing it. He knew a lot more than he told us about many things." My father scanned the courtyard again before continuing.

"We're already seeing pressure from Ainsworth to do things we don't want to do. They're testing our resolve now that Warvold is gone. And it's no secret that Pervis is getting further out of control at a time when we need his leadership." My father leaned forward with his elbows on his knees and began picking at his fingernails.

"Warvold talked about you all the time, about your obvious interest in the outside and how smart you were for your age. He saw a lot of the adventurer he once was in you, and he mentioned more than once how unfortunate it was that you were locked inside the walls he built. He understood why you liked to sneak around by yourself." My father paused and turned to look at me.

"Did he tell you anything that night when he died?" It was an accusing question, and it startled me.

"No, nothing important. He acted very strange though. He reminisced about the past and told me a silly fable about blind men, but that was all," I said.

My father watched me carefully as I spoke, trying to see if I was telling the truth or not. He didn't ask about the key and I didn't tell. It was too precious to give up without being asked about it directly. He sighed deeply, went back to picking his nails, and continued.

"People are worried down in Turlock, and they want Ganesh and I to make a visit. We're leaving this morning and we'll be gone for two days. I know it's sudden, but these are troubled times and we're trying to keep things under control. I'll give Pervis a leave in Ainsworth while we're gone so you won't kill each other." He paused again and looked at me as if sure I would be a nuisance while he was gone.

"I've spoken to Grayson and he will look after you. Can I count on you to stay out of trouble, at least until I get back?"

I chose my reply carefully. "I've already had enough trouble for one visit to Bridewell."

My answer seemed to satisfy him. We stood and hugged briefly, then he started to walk away from me towards Renny Lodge. A moment later he was gone, and I stood alone at the center of town, the walls of Bridewell towering all around me.

Somehow I felt more like a prisoner than I had before.

CABEZA DE VACA

It was nine in the morning when I left my room for the second time that day. I wore a leather pouch around my neck. In it I placed the map, the key, and my pocketknife. My mother had brought me a sweater during the funeral, which I tied around my waist. I took nothing else with me, thinking even if I was lucky I would only be gone for a few hours.

When I arrived in the library I removed the map and began searching for a starting place. It was much more difficult than I thought it would be to decipher the locations. The map only showed the winding paths, no sign of doors, walls, or windows. From my low vantage point I could not see what the pattern looked like. It was clear only that the mountain on the map was along one of the four edges of the large room. It struck me as odd that Grayson would understand the map at first glance like he did, but then he was here day in and day out for years and years and had walked each aisle thousands of times. I was only here a few days a year. Still, I was thoroughly confused.

Every time I started down a twisting aisle of books that seemed to look like one on the map, it turned out to be a different path all together. It was almost as if the map was changing as I was looking at it. I turned it every which way, started from different walls and entryways, but all my effort led me around in circles.

After an hour, I wandered into Grayson's office to see if he would make a midmorning run to the kitchen with me. He was hunkered down over a beautiful green and yellow book, using gold leaf paint to fill in some missing spots on the cover. My stomach rumbled and he looked up from his work.

"I was just thinking the same thing," he said, and we meandered down the hall together making small talk. We were mostly quiet as we sat in the kitchen drinking cold milk and eating strawberry jam on buns, and then I removed the map and set it on the table.

"See if you can guess where my favorite chair is on this map," I said, hoping for some insight that would help me find my way.

I turned the map towards Grayson and he looked thoughtfully at it. He seemed to be having as much trouble as I was at first, then his brows went up, and in his haste, he used a jammy index finger to poke the map where he thought my chair would be. It left a sticky red spot on an otherwise clean map, and he apologized, but I didn't mind. Grayson had just put a giant red dot on the mountain. Now that I saw it, everything shifted into place on the map. I realized where Grayson's office and the doors into the library were, along with the windows and the rolling pathways of books. It all made sense.

I could tell Grayson was likely to eat a lot more food and take his time getting back to work, so it was the perfect opportunity to duck out. "Thanks for the company, Grayson. I'll catch up with you later." As I stood to go, I added, "I'm going to be busy with something for the next few days, so if you don't see me there's nothing to worry about."

Grayson nodded and I walked out of the kitchen, which was about what I had expected. In all the years I had been coming to Bridewell, my father never thought to investigate what sort of chaperone Grayson was. In times past when my father left for one or two days, he would always ask Grayson to take care of me, and Grayson was always happy to do it. Only Grayson never adjusted his behavior after the request. I'd see him in the library or maybe I wouldn't. If I didn't cross his path for an entire day and night, Grayson thought nothing of it. I think the walls made him, and probably my father as well, very lax with supervision. After all, how far could I go?

I ran back to the library and zigzagged my way through the maze of aisles. Rounding a sharp corner, I bumped my shoulder on a bookcase and nearly sent rows of books crashing to the floor. I steadied the teetering shelf and continued on, my run toned down to a brisk walk. Before I knew it, I was standing in front of my favorite old chair. A hawk sat outside the windowsill, and did not stir as I came into view. Then both cats were on the chair, watching me intently. It was weird how all three remained still and alert, following my every move.

I started by feeling along the wall and the sill, and then on the shelves near the chair, which were covered with books. I felt every nook and dimple carefully and pulled out a lot of old books I'd looked at before. I began to think that maybe a certain one might trigger a secret passage or reveal a hidden treasure. Before long, I had taken almost all the books out and placed them in teetering piles around me. This exercise produced a lot of dust but nothing of any interest, although the cats did enjoy chasing one another around and darting between stacks.

I put all the books back one at a time, and ten minutes later I flopped down in the chair, tired and frustrated. I looked over my shoulder and realized that the chair was pushed up against the only wall I had not checked, a wall that was a structural part of a staircase on the other side. I got up and pulled on the chair, a heavy beast that clearly had not been moved for a long time. It took all my strength to slowly budge it out into the open space.

With the chair out of the way, I could see an otherwise covered section of the wood wall, with its paneled dark brown accents. Just below the middle trim, dead center where the back of the chair had been was a small green figure of a mountain. I ran my fingers over the image and felt a dimple at its center, though I could see no change in appearance. I took the silver key out of my pocket and held it in my shaking hand. I looked over my shoulder and saw the cats perched in the top edge of the chair watching me. "You two are awfully curious today," I said. Looking over them I saw the hawk in the sill. "So is your feathered friend there at the window. Do you all know something I don't?" I said it half expecting an answer, but I only received a blank stare from all three, along with a wimpy meow from Sam.

I felt again for the dimple, put the key to it, and watched as it slid into the wall. Then I turned the key and heard a light *click*. I removed the key and placed it back in my leather pouch, and then I quickly looked around to make sure nobody was watching. I pushed against the wall with one hand and a panel, about two feet by two feet, slid open on creaking hinges. A soft whip of cool, earthy air escaped, running over my face like a faint whisper.

With the light pouring in from the library I could see a ladder going down into the dark and the underside of the stairs above. An old oil lamp, complete with a small box of wooden matches, hung from a rusty nail on the third step of the ladder. I could only see the first six rungs going down and the first few feet of planks covering the walls. After that, the hole was swallowed by a deathly still blackness.

The cool air continued to work its way slowly out of the small doorway as if a frozen, sleeping giant was breathing steadily through the hole. It smelled like the dusty road to Bridewell just after a heavy rain had given it a good soaking. I turned to the bookshelf on my right and browsed through the items at eye level. I chose the smallest one I could find, a little red covered volume with white lettering in the spine. *Adventures at the Border of the Tenth City* by someone with a strange name whom I'd never heard of. I opened the book and read the first page and I was immediately captivated by the audacious subject matter.

Cabeza de Vaca was an explorer who left his home in The Northern Kingdom during the 7th reign of Blackwell.

After surviving a hurricane near Mount Laythen he turned back and headed toward the great ravine, where he was trapped for a week in a cave by a relentless pack of wolves. When at last the wolves conceded, a hungry and tired Cabeza continued his journey into The Sly Field.

Cabeza lived on what he could find and traveled among the oddities of The Sly Field (of which there are many), searching for a way through the mist and into the mythical Tenth City. But each time he tried to enter the mist it so covered everything around him he could scarcely see his own hand in front of his face. And so each time he wandered about for days in the shroud of that place, and always he came out near the same spot he'd gone in.

Eventually he gave up his quest for The Tenth City and went instead to Mount Norwood where he wrote of his travels. This book is an account of Cabeza de Vaca's adventures in The Great Ravine, The Sly Field, and the mists that lie ahead of The Tenth City.

According to chapter titles for the book, it would go on to talk about his role in the government of the Northern Kingdoms, his later travels, and eventual death.

I closed the book and held it in my hand. "For a man with the head of a cow, you didn't do too badly for yourself." It was common for me to talk to authors this way; somehow it made them more real.

"Your travels are about to include one flight to the bottom of a creepy black pit." I held the book out over the opening and let go, sending Cabeza de Vaca free falling into darkness.

It took a lot longer then I had hoped it would for the book to hit bottom. Not being a scientist, I lacked the ability to calculate the time, speed, and distance of the event, but my best guess put the bottom of the hole in the neighborhood of thirty terrifying feet. It was hard to imagine what I would encounter at the bottom. Maybe there actually was a sleeping giant waiting for a tasty young lady to warm his belly.

I turned and looked back into the library. The hawk remained, but the cats were nowhere to be seen. I stood up and tried to scare the bird off, flashing my arms out and banging my feet on the floor, but the hawk sat silent and still, eyes fixated on my every move.

I crouched down, reached into the darkness, and took the lamp from the nail. The glass that protected the wick was jammed and I had to force it off. I wetted the wick with oil from the basin, then broke two matches before successfully striking the third. My lighting problem solved, I turned back to the passageway.

The eerie dark breeze remained. It made my lamp flicker and sent faint shadows across the walls. I hung my feet over the edge and swung them out onto the ladder, then I slithered through the hole and caught hold of the top rung with my left hand. I took the lamp in my other hand and hung it by the old rusty nail. Only one thing left to do, seal myself in, so no one would know where I'd gone. I reached back into the library and grabbed the leg of the chair, then I moved it in little spurts as I lunged back again and again on the ladder. With the chair in place I swung the secret door shut from the inside and it clicked into position. The locking mechanism was simple to use from the backside, but I clicked it in and out several times to be sure. I took the lamp and hung it down as low as I could, re-hanging it on the fifth rung. I stepped down the ladder and repeated this process until I was standing on a dirt floor, twenty-eight rungs under ground.

Looking up was much like looking down had been, the light evaporating into a starless black sky after only a few feet. There were walls on three sides and a tunnel heading west under the library in the direction of the mountains. The book I had dropped lay on the ground. Cow head had landed badly, and it appeared I now had two items in my possession that would require Grayson's attention. I was destroying books at an alarming pace.

One last look up, and then I started walking westward under the city. The walls were made of wood planks with earth peeking through at the seams; the floor was packed dirt. I passed old footprints, which sent my heart racing and even made me turn back for home. I told myself over and over again that I was the only one in the tunnel, and eventually I began walking toward the mountains again. The tunnel did not change in height or width as I walked on, but my trek went uphill at an unexpectedly steep grade. After ten minutes, about the time it takes to walk from one side of Bridewell to the other at a steady pace, the tunnel began to turn slightly to the right, then it straightened out and I walked at least as far again.

After a while I reached the end, a wall jutting straight up in front of me, another ladder hanging down, a familiar hollow blackness dripping on me from above. I was afraid to climb, and I imagined the sharp teeth of the giant closing on me if I went up into his gaping mouth. I was sweaty and tired, and I sat down in the dirt at the base of the ladder to rest before going up.

"Hey cow head, how are you doing?" I said to the book in my hand. I wiped my brow against my shirt and looked back down the tunnel toward home. "Were there times you got scared and thought you might not make it? I bet there were. I bet you had those kinds of thoughts all the time.

"I think I'll have to leave you here now, since you really provide no practical value for the rest of my journey, which will probably end on the tongue of a giant at the top of this ladder. You wait here for me, and if I make it back, I promise I'll read all about you." I had to give him points for listening;

he was an obedient cow, if not a very talkative one.

I stood up, faced the ladder, and began my climb. Twenty-eight rungs later, I bumped my head on boards at the top, and pushed with all my might to budge them out of the way. With no warning at all, the whole top flew up in the air, blinding me with intense light that made me close my stinging eyes. Bits of dirt fell down onto my face and head. I nearly lost my grip and fell into the hole. The lamp dangled precariously off the top rung and went out.

It was quiet except for noises I had only heard from a distance before; a breeze dancing through the trees, birds singing, bushes rustling all around me. I was terrified to emerge from my crouch on the ladder and look over the edge where the top had been blown off. Again, I contemplated turning back and running down the tunnel. I decided I would take a peek, and if it was scary, I would hustle down the ladder as fast as my feet could carry me.

I slowly moved up and looked over the edge, and to my great surprise, the hawk was sitting on a large stone a few feet away, looking just as it had when I'd left the library.

"Well now, you are a small one, aren't you?" I turned quickly in the direction of the voice behind me. Balancing the trap door he had just pulled open was the smallest man I have ever seen. He could not have stood more than two feet. "They were right about that much, you're a little bugger, definitely small enough," the man said. The trap door wobbled back and forth with the push of a light breeze and the overcorrecting pull from the man. If it came crashing down, it would smack my head and send me falling like a rock to the dirt floor.

"I'll be needing you to come on out of there right quick. I can't hold this door up much longer." And then the small man gave a nod to the hawk, and it was gone in a flash of feathers and screeching. "Darius will be pleased I've found you. With some luck, we'll be in the forest by midmorning tomorrow as he had hoped." I was out of the hole and on my feet, confused and not sure what I should do next.

The small man pushed the door down and it slammed hard against the ground. It was covered with moss and it had a long thin rope made of braided tree bark attached to the top edge.

"We can't stay out here in the open. Must be moving along. We have a ways to go and hard climbing it is," said the little man, and he was leaving me behind, walking at a brisk pace away from me into the mountains. He glanced back with a scolding look on his face. "Well, come on Alexa!"

"Wait! Who are you? How did you know my name? Come back!" But the small man just kept on walking, and so I followed, racing to catch up.

He yelled back at me, continuing on, not looking back. "My name is Yipes. I live in the mountains, and I am here to take you to your appointed destination."

I looked back over my shoulder and saw the wall getting smaller and smaller in the distance. I was surprised at how insignificant it looked, cowering at the foot of the mountains. Beyond the walls the Dark Hills rolled on and on, into ominous and forbidding valleys unseen from Bridewell itself. I turned to the mountains and began walking again. The higher I went, the higher they seemed to go, ever farther and brighter in the sunlight, ever expanding to places I could never fully discover. I stopped and turned to look upon Bridewell again, and I saw it as I had never seen it before. It sat squarely between darkness and light, its roads a three-headed snake, bound at the center with a hideous head, dividing vast lands. It had a certain balance, a symmetry—as if each land were pushing against the walls, trying to bring them down, to dominate, and to rule. As I began walking again, following the little man, I felt a profound sense of exhilaration and fear, and I promised myself never to venture out into The Dark Hills no matter what duty might call me into its sinister lands.

CHAPTER II

THE GLOWING POOL

Yipes was a fast walker for such a small man, and keeping pace with him was hard work. My feet were blistering and my shoulders and cheeks were burned and tender to the touch. Sweat dripped down my nose and stung my eyes. I kept looking back as we climbed higher into the mountains, the wall diminishing into a lifeless, stringy worm in the distance.

Yipes was not the talkative sort, or at least he was quiet during our trek. At first, I asked him questions, but his lack of response and my exhaustion eventually wore me down, and we worked our way up the mountain in the heat of the day in relative silence. Now and then we would pass under a grouping of trees where the shade felt cool and leaves rustled high in branches beyond my view.

Watching Yipes scamper in front of me like a rabbit, it struck me that I was following a small, strange man into the wild. I might never return to my home, never see my parents or friends again, and never wander the rows of books in the Bridewell library. Even so, the reality of being outside the wall and the rush of the adventure were feelings that somehow comforted me. I felt as if I was doing what I was meant to do, and I knew no fear, no regret, and no need to consume my mind with thoughts of home or family.

I don't know how long I was lost in my thoughts, but I

nearly stumbled right over the top of Yipes who had stopped and turned in my direction. If not for his cry of "whoa, young lady!" I might have put my knee right into his plump little nose. I crouched down to get a better look at him and take advantage of a rare chance to confront my guide face to face. He had dark eyes, a dainty mustache, and slight lips before a row of yellowy teeth. His skin was dark and leathery, toasty brown like he'd been taking heat from the sun in large doses for quite some time. He wore a tan colored hat over flowing brown hair, leather shorts, a simple top, and leather sandals.

"Thank you for stopping. I thought you might go on all day. You're quite the climber, aren't you?" I said.

Chin high, chest out, with a comic high voice, Yipes answered me, "I'm not allowed to talk to you just now, sorry, so sorry. I wish I could. Strict orders from Darius." And then, looking all around him and leaning close to my face he said, "thank you for the compliment." He seemed completely harmless, casually standing in the middle of the path, a slight grin on his face.

"Can you tell me where we're going or who this Darius you keep talking about is? We've been climbing for an awfully long time and I have no idea where you're taking me," I said.

He was back at attention now, stiff and serious. "Sorry, strictest orders. I must take you to the appointed destination as quickly as possible. Important meeting tomorrow, very important mee—" He stopped short, turned his cantaloupe-sized head to the left, and listened intently. In a flash he was through the bushes and scaling a nearby tree like a spooked squirrel. Seconds later he was so high in the branches of the tree I lost sight of him. I moved from side to side trying to find him in the tree, but I had lost him. I looked back down the mountain and saw the thin, endless snakes of the walls far below. I imagined I could flick them with my finger and knock them all down.

When I turned back to the trail Yipes was standing at attention, not winded in the slightest, with the same calm manner as before. "So sorry. I thought I heard something in the bushes. Can't be too careful now, can we? Important cargo. Yes, very important cargo." He led me to a stream where we drank. I began gulping and Yipes told me to drink only a little or I might become ill and weak. He gave me dried meat from his pouch and told me to sit and rest. Another sip of the icy water and a few minutes more rest, then we were off again.

"Not far now. Not far at all," said Yipes as we meandered farther up the mountain, our pace much faster than it had been. The trees grew thick, but the heat remained stifling as we approached mid afternoon. Lost in my thoughts, the minutes turned into another hour of treading time behind my stalwart companion. My feet ached with open blisters, and my legs burned with every step, but I was determined to keep going without complaint.

The stream we had rested at earlier now ran alongside of us and we walked its bank. Only a few feet wide with a bright green underbelly, it was full with the refreshing sound of water flowing over rocks. I saw flashes here and there in its depths; fish moving and reflecting as they sensed our presence along the edge. I was so tired I thought I might pass out, and again I lost track of Yipes in my delirious wondering.

"Excuse me. You can stop now," said Yipes. He was sitting on a large rock a few feet behind me, lacing his leather sandal, which had come undone. He looked annoyingly refreshed, as if the massive trek we had just made was nothing more than a sightseeing stroll around Bridewell.

"I'm afraid this is as far as I can take you. The rest you have to do on your own," said Yipes, now lapping up water from the stream, which had shrunk to only a couple of feet across.

I hobbled over to the stream, now quiet in its slow movement, and I drank in large gulps until I thought I would burst. Then I sat at the water's edge and felt it all coming back up again. Hunching over, soupy water poured out of my mouth. I fought off a sickly shiver, rinsed my mouth in the stream, and turned to face Yipes. Exhausted, I lurched forward and fell on my face.

Why am I out here in the dark? Something warm is beside me. Warvold, his mouth gaping, rotted teeth dripping yellow goo down his chin. He's grabbing me by the shoulder, shaking me hard. Run, Alexa, run! Get away!

"Wake up Alexa, wake up now. You must get on with it." Yipes was gently nudging my shoulder with his clam-sized hand. It was late afternoon, maybe four o'clock. I must have slept for at least an hour. I stretched, let out a painful sigh, pulled my knees to my chest, and sat breathing heavy sobs, tears rolling down my knee caps, running a wet track to the top of my feet. My body ached all over, and my mind continued to struggle with the surroundings. I had an unfortunate dull throb in my head. It felt like a man, one even smaller than Yipes, was standing behind my eyeballs with a club, swinging with all his might to bang his way out.

Bang, bang, bang! 'Sorry Mr. Yipes sir, she won't budge!' 'Put your back into it man! Give it all you've got!' Bang, bang, bang!

"Alexa, stop that now! Pounding your head against your knees won't make you feel any better. On that you can trust me," said Yipes. "Come on then, on your feet!" He was in the stream now, splashing me with icy cold water. I jerked awake, jumping to a stand, and felt the shearing pain in my legs and feet. The open blisters were screaming back at me to sit down. *Sit down or I'll send the club through your forehead!* I fell to my knees; Yipes continued the chilling barrage of splashes until I finally screamed.

"Enough! I'm up, just give me a second and I'll be ready to start walking again." He stopped splashing and watched me as I rung my hair out with my hands. Then he emerged from the stream and returned to his perch on the rock. I was back on my feet, gaining more confidence that I might have the strength to hobble my weary bones a few more steps into the mountains.

"I think I'm ready for another hour or two. You're going to have to slow down though; I'm nursing some remarkable blisters," I said.

Yipes smiled and sat with his elbows on his knees, hands folded, and spoke in a soft, slow voice: "Young lady, like I told you before, we've arrived. You're an impressive climber. For a child, and such a small one at that, you did very well," he said.

"Now, it is my duty and my privilege to point you in the direction of your destiny. My work is done for now. I've brought you this far, but the next bit of effort is all yours I'm afraid. What I need you to do is walk up this stream. Get right in the water and walk until you reach a pool. You'll know it when you see it, trust me on that one. This is a special place. You only get one chance to go there in all your life. I cannot tell you what to do when you get there. That you must figure out on your own."

I looked up the stream with its bright green bed. It disappeared from view around a corner into the trees a hundred feet away. "But how will I know when I've arrived in the right spo— " I turned back to look at Yipes, and found the rock bare.

I removed my sandals and held them in my hand, dangling them from the straps with my fingers. My feet ached more than ever on the hot sandy dirt at the edge of the stream, so I immediately staggered into the water. The stream was only a few feet wide, and it came to my knees in the middle. It felt cold on my bare legs. My feet felt the heavenly touch of the soft furry bottom. It was like walking on a perfect feathery pillow, only better because the mossy green came up between my toes and surrounded my feet with a delicate squishy wrapper. I let out a thankful 'ahhhh' and an unexpected smile sprouted onto my face. In the heat of the day I dunked my head and body the rest of the way in and exploded out of the stream refreshed and walking, enjoying the velvet whisper of every step on my swollen feet.

The stream narrowed further as I rounded the corner, but it remained a foot deep. The water moved slowly and quietly. As I walked farther and rounded yet another corner, I saw a pool surrounded by rock walls on all sides except for the direction I was coming from. This was the place.

I reached the edge of the pool, which was about ten feet across on all sides. I looked down and found that the water had turned to a murky brown around my legs. Behind me, where I had been walking, an inky darkness inhabited the stream like a plague of locusts in a summer sky. The pool itself glowed in a strange hue I had never seen before. I moved to its center in three quick strides, and for a brief moment I could see the bottom, the water now at my chest. I saw the shimmering outline of a robin's egg stone bursting with lavish green color. A moment later, my disturbance in the pool brought up a muddy brown thickness around my legs, settling around my chest and leaving me almost chin deep in dirty water.

I dove down, grabbed a handful of rocks, and brought them up into the air. They were all brown and bland, entirely void of bright color. Had I been dreaming? I dove down again and again, all over the pool until I was exhausted and angry, standing in a dark pool of icky guck.

I slapped my arms against the water with a loud pop and let out a grunt of frustration. "I don't understand! What am I supposed to do in here?" I yelled, hoping to see Yipes climb down the rock wall with an answer. But I was utterly alone. As I stood motionless in the water the blackness seemed to turn a shade lighter. Maybe if I could stay completely still the gook and dirt would settle down enough so that I could see the glowing emerald rock clearly again. Then, if I reached down ever so slowly, maybe I could pick out the right rock and it would be glowing green in my hand. While it may not be the end of the test, it seemed like a good place to start, and so I stood, still as a statue, in a pool of murky water, patiently waiting.

It took a lot longer than I thought it might for the water to change. It stayed just the same for an excruciatingly long time. Was it a lighter shade of brown? Could I see the outline of shapes at the bottom of the pool? I couldn't be sure, and I continued to wait and wait. It felt an awful lot like when I stood on the sill in my room for hours on end looking out the window for a sign of life in The Dark Hills. I wondered how father and Ganesh and everyone else was doing. I missed them terribly. This and a thousand other random thoughts filled my head as I tried my best to stay perfectly motionless.

The water was definitely getting lighter now. Unfortunately, the day was getting darker almost as fast. The water had been exhilarating at first, but I was starting to shiver as the heat of the day began to wane. Surely my feet were prunes by now, and worse, my arches were precariously close to cramping, which would cause me to move and stir up the water all over again. Night was coming, and with it a cruel coldness that would force me out of the pool.

I closed my eyes and concentrated hard. I imagined I was sitting next to my father, he with his pipe billowing sweet smoke around the room. The fire was a raging monster, stacked high with crackling wood, sending an orange shimmer across the faces in the room; Ganesh, Grayson, Silas Hardy, Nicolas, plus my father, all ranting in their usual way: that rancid tobacco is about as welcome as a skunk at a dinner party, you think the sun comes up just to hear you crow, and other such nonsense that made the evening flow like thick honey into the wee hours.

I opened my eyes and looked up. It was night in the sky, stars sparkling in clusters across my line of sight. And yet it was not dark as the dark of an unlit night ought to be, the way the streets of Bridewell were after the lamps are extinguished and all is black but for the dim lamplight at the towers. The three rock walls shimmered unnaturally, like the pages of a book under flitting candle light. I gazed along the wall, and down into the water below me. The pool was aglow with radiant green light, pulsing from a single thumb sized rock a few inches from my big toe. My feet and legs reflected the fuzzy lime flame, which worked its diminishing magic to the edges of the pool in a soft, smoldering finish.

My shivering was rabid now; goaded on by the dreaded thought of reaching down into the water, submerging my head, neck, and shoulders in the icy glow. The more I shivered, the weaker the glow became, and I could see that if I waited much longer, the dirt would rise again and put out the light from the stone entirely. I slowly descended to my neck, yelping in slow bursts as the sting of cold took my breath away. Then I gulped a big breath of air, held it against my will, and plunged all the way under.

I could see the stone clearly now, surrounded by other stones that remained brown and black and lifeless. It was just the one, the one by my big toe that shown like a tiny green sun in a liquid sky. I reached down slowly and grasped its warm surface in my hand; then rose, blasting out of the water, my body frozen in the night air.

"Well done little lady." It was the unmistakable high-pitched voice of Yipes. "Come on out of there now, I don't want you catching a cold."

I was smiling through my chattering teeth, delighted at the sight of my little friend hanging by the stone wall a few feet above me like a monkey on a tree trunk. He climbed around the wall and down to the streams edge a few feet away, motioning me repeatedly with his arm.

"I'm f-f-f-rozen Y-y-yipes!" I hobbled as best I could out of the pool and onto the mossy edge of the stream. I was greeted with a warm blanket, which I eagerly wrapped around my shoulders as I sat on the soft dry bank. Out of the confines of the pool, we were drenched in a welcome bath of moonlight.

"Where are your shoes?" said Yipes as he placed a leather string around my neck with a pouch at the end.

I cursed, surprising Yipes and myself with the outburst. "I must have dropped them in the p-p-pool. I had them in my hand when I went in, but I've l-l-lost them now," I said.

"No worries, no worries. Put the gem in the pouch around your neck. I'll be right back." Before I could protest he was gone, head first into the water and out of sight. Then with a *whoosh*! He was out of the water at the center of the pool, holding my sandals over his head. "These yours?" he said, with a grin on his face, water dripping down his mustache.

He swam back and held my sandals out to me, but I was busy turning the stone in my hands. It maintained a radiant glow. It was smooth, about half the size of a chicken egg, and heavier than it ought to have been for its size. The color was astonishing, a tasty lime cream that made me want to smell it expecting a tart zing in my nostrils.

"Still holding that thing?" asked Yipes. "You really should put it in the pouch for safekeeping. That's one stone you don't want to lose." And so I did, pulling it tightly shut after dropping it into its new home, a dry, coarse chamber very different from its previous watery environment. I found myself strangely concerned for its well-being.

"The thing is to keep moving now. I know your feet are hurting you, but the worst is over. Just a little bit farther and you can take a break," said Yipes, wet from head to toe but standing at attention without a sign of discomfort.

I was up without complaint and ready to go. Yipes was starting to grow on me and I was happy to follow his orders if he wouldn't leave me behind. We walked away from the stream into the silence of the night, the moon lighting our way, Renny Lodge somewhere off in the distant hallow of evening.

DARIUS

After Yipes and I had walked for half an hour, I heard the sound of fast moving water. We approached a stream, which was about twenty feet wide. It held fat, formless boulders along its sides and through its middle like freckles on the descending arm of a giant mountain creature. On the other side of the stream, the moon shone down on an odd little house, leaning precariously on stilts, half over the water and half on land. It was small, and jutted three miniature stories into the night sky. Puffs of smoke rose from its chimney.

Yipes hopped a path of boulders across the stream, and I followed dutifully to the other side, half enjoying the challenge and half scared I might feel the cold sting of a misplaced footing. He was across and awaiting my arrival before I reached the third of twelve boulders.

"You're a decent hopper," he said as I jumped down from my last rock. "And you followed my path exactly. That's good, very good. A talent such as that will come in handy."

He turned and walked up the path towards the odd three-story house. I followed him, curious what the inside would look like. The nearby stream persisted with its pleasant, crisp sound. We came to the front porch and Yipes stopped. Perched on the ledge of the porch rail was the hawk, and Yipes gave it a soft scratch on the neck.

"This is my house, Alexa. I'll accommodate you as best I can until morning, then Darius will be here to take you to the meeting," he said, and he opened the door, which stood about three feet tall and a foot and a half wide.

I had to enter on my knees with my shoulders turned sideways, but I only stood four and a half feet tall myself, so it wasn't as bad as I thought it might be. I imagined Grayson trying to get in, sucking his gut tight, mercilessly wedged like a cork with his plump belly against the door jams; or Pervis Kotcher crouched inside the front room and turning his behind into the fireplace, banging his head against the low rafters as he hooped and howled. Once inside, I took the room to be on the order of twelve feet side-to-side, four feet from floor to ceiling.

It was cozy and warm, even though I had to remain seated to avoid hitting my head. There was a table at the center of the room, which was filled with bread, nuts, fruit, and fresh water. I hadn't thought of food all day, but seeing the spread in front of me made my stomach quake with hunger. "Yipes can I—"

"No need to ask. You are my honored guest; the food is for you, of course," and he licked his lips and brushed his mustache with his hand.

"I refuse to eat unless you join me in the feast," I said.

"Well, I suppose if you insist," he said, pulling a wonderful little nutcracker out of his pocket and advancing on the table. A broad smile covered his face, hiding his mouth almost entirely with the delicate fuzz from his mustache.

I reclined on my elbow and he sat at the table on a rickety wooden chair. We ate our fill while the warm glow of the fire danced on the walls. A spiral staircase wound up to the second floor, but it was clear I would have difficulty making the climb. By the looks of it, there was a reasonable chance of altogether lodging myself in the passageway, so I decided not to ask if I could see the rest of his fine little home. Instead, I probed him with questions.

"You're sworn to secrecy, not a word about this man Darius out of you, or the mysterious meeting I'm to attend?" I asked, already well into a large, juicy apple.

"Soon enough you'll know everything, soon enough indeed."

"Can you tell me why you live in the mountains and where you came from?" I asked.

He puzzled awhile, fiddling with his nutcracker, then cleaned out a walnut shell. Nibbling its contents, he offered: "I can't tell you much, not allowed I'm afraid. I did live in Bridewell for a time, a long while ago. My parents left me on the streets in a town far away from here when they realized I was never going to grow to a normal size." He paused, then added: "You can disappear easily when nobody notices you to begin with." Crack, he was busy on another walnut.

"I'm small, and I can't disappear easily at all," I said.

"Well now, that's because you're special. You're small, but very special indeed."

I think we talked a while longer, but the heat of the room and my full stomach made me so tired, I really can't remember how I got on the floor or when I began sleeping. I only remember waking up, the room in the early glow of morning, crisp and cool. I was crumpled up on the floor like a baby, and a blanket was over my body. A quilted pillow nestled my head. I was half asleep, half awake.

She's bigger than I thought she would be.

Oh, she's just fine. Even I can see that.

All right, All right. No need to get excited. She'll do just fine, I agree. You've done a wonderful job getting her this far.

She did it all by herself. No help needed from the likes of me. She's the one you want. She's the one.

The voices became clearer and I sat up. For a timeless moment I thought I was in my room at Renny Lodge and everything I had experienced the previous day had merely been a dream. Then I did a spastic crab walk back against the wall as I turned and saw a full-grown wolf standing next to Yipes, razor sharp white teeth an inch long in its panting mouth.

I sat motionless, my back against the wall, and felt a familiar cold fear digging into my bones. I rubbed my eyes to make sure I was awake, and found with unfortunate clarity that I was indeed alert and fully conscious. Then I began to feel a strange awareness all around me. It felt as though I somehow understood what the trees were saying as the wind blew through the branches outside, and what the water rolling over the rocks in the stream meant to express.

"Allow me to introduce myself. I am Darius," said the wolf. His lips did not move to speak like a human, but I comprehended him entirely. The way he moved from side to side, his paws shuffling on the floor. The tilt of his head, the subtle noises from his throat, and a hundred other things combined to form a language I understood with perfect accuracy. What was happening to me?

"I'm sorry, did I just hear you introduce yourself?" I said.

"Yes you did. And I understand you are Alexa Daley of Bridewell Common. I am ever so pleased to make your acquaintance," said the wolf.

"Likewise," I said in a flat, quiet tone.

Yipes said nothing and remained stiff at attention against the far wall. The wolf advanced in liquid strides and stopped a few feet in front of me.

"I know you're confused and in need of answers. I also know that you only have today and tomorrow before you must return to Bridewell. I know about your father, Grayson, Ganesh, and Pervis Kotcher. I know about your mother, about Nicolas, about Warvold, and a great many other things you don't know about.

"You have been chosen for a special purpose, Alexa. The

birth of Warvold set in motion events that his death must now bring to a close. He chose you to accomplish this task, and you it must be.

"Yipes has been kind enough to bring you this far. Now, it is my duty to escort you to a meeting with the forest ruler and his council. I can take you as far as the Lathbury tunnel where you will continue your journey with Malcolm. He will take you the rest of the way."

Forest ruler, council, more tunnels—my head swam with facts I could not begin to comprehend. Naturally, my first instinct was to back out of any false sense of duty I might have stumbled into.

"But I'm just a child—a *small* child. I can get my father, he'll believe me; you can talk to him about whatever you need," I protested.

"Alexa." It was Yipes whispering from across the room. I could barely hear him utter my name.

He continued in a soft voice, "your size is your strength, without it you could not have been chosen. Look at me; I'm half your size. And yet without me, you would still be bumping your head against a tunnel door, locked away inside Bridewell. The size of your body is just right, Alexa. The only question is whether you're big enough *inside*."

Then Darius added, "By nightfall, I promise, everything will be clear, and I'll have you on your way home by morning."

I looked at Yipes and longed to sit with him and chat the day away. He was standing at perfect attention, letting a tear run down his cheek without wiping it away.

"All right, I'll go," I said, and I understood the broad, sweet smile of a wild wolf. It was clear that Darius was in a rush to get things moving along, for just as soon as I agreed to the meeting he was next to me, nudging me towards the door with his powerful head.

"Will I see you again?" I asked Yipes, as we made our

way out the door and off the porch. He was hanging a satchel packed with dried food around my neck.

"I think so child," he said, tears welling up again in his eyes. "Darius will take good care of you. You can trust him." Then he was tending to his hawk, embarrassed and turned away from me. I ran back and picked him up like a big stuffed doll and hugged him. Then I spun him in a circle and set him back down on his porch. Without another look back I began walking with Darius, the sound of the stream farther and farther away, until it was lost in the rustle of the trees overhead.

THE TERRIBLE SECRET

I had the distinct feeling we were going the wrong way. I knew the general location of the wall and the three gated roads, and I was almost sure we were heading toward the Lunenburg road, which was opposite from where we should have been going. The road to Lunenburg split the mountains from The Dark Hills, not the mountains from the forest.

"Darius?" I said.

"Yes, Alexa, what is it?"

"I haven't as keen a sense of direction as you must have, but it seems to me we're heading in the wrong direction."

"Very good, Alexa. You are correct. We're making a slight detour before the meeting. Something I need you to see that won't take but a moment."

Darius was a friendly enough sort, but he had not mentioned this unscheduled diversion when we were with Yipes; it made me suspicious and edgy. Besides, he was a wolf, and I was a lost and helpless sheep. I would keep my guard up, and if things continued to feel wrong, I would cut off the trail and go back to find Yipes.

Darius was a big wolf, not at all like the small ones I'd seen in books. On all fours he reached my shoulders, and his head was the size of the ripe watermelons in my mother's garden. His thick salt and pepper coat looked soft and full, though I'd not had the occasion to touch it. Placed against my hand, his massive paws would surely run the full distance of my fingers and thumb. His powerful jaws looked as though they could cut through a wagon wheel.

"Here we are," he said.

"Where is here?" I asked, apprehensive about what the answer would be. Then I looked past Darius and realized we were standing in a thicket, with only twenty yards between the Lunenburg road and us.

"How far to the right is the Lunenburg gate?" I questioned.

"Not far, about two hundred yards. But we're safely tucked away where the guards cannot see us. And besides, we've got hawks doing double duty this morning. They will let us know if danger is anywhere nearby."

"Why have you brought me here Darius, to test me? To see if I'll run for the tower and tell everyone the animals can talk and this place really *is* haunted?"

"Goodness me no! They would think you were crazy. Besides, they can't understand us, only you can." he said.

Darius continued, "There was a tunnel carved a long while ago that goes under this wall. It's small, almost too small for me to fit—and anyway I can't stand tunnels and I refuse to go in them, no matter the size.

"The tunnel is about a hundred yards long, and it goes gradually deeper into the ground. At the end is a row of wood planks, and on the other side of the wood planks is packed dirt, though I'm told there is a spot where you can see through if you look just right. Badgers built the tunnel, and Yipes constructed the planks and packed dirt at the end. He's smaller than you and spent a lot of time down there working.

"You must crawl down to the end before I take you to Malcolm. It's the one other thing you must do." Darius stepped aside, and indeed there was a small hole, about two feet around, staring up at me.

"I'm not sure I can fit in that hole," I said, even though I was nearly positive I could.

Darius walked a few paces until he was standing in the shade at the base of a large tree. He lay down and closed his eyes, his large head resting on soft front paws. "You were chosen because you are small, Alexa. I think you'll fit." Then he was quiet, breathing steadily, as though he had fallen asleep.

I peered down into the hole, and I was unhappy to find it going dark rather quickly. Was I expected to climb down into a dark hole and stumble into a den of badgers, thrashing and clawing until they tore me to shreds in a silent underground grave? Darius could be plotting to have me killed for any number of reasons. I barely knew him, and he was the *only* wolf I knew. Could I trust a wolf? What if he was a bad wolf? Weren't they all bad? I looked over at Darius, who appeared to be perfectly content to nap the morning away in the shade of the trees.

It was true I could run, straight for the tower screaming and yelling and throwing my arms around. Or I might be able to find my way back to the secret tunnel leading to the library. That was a bit more of a stretch, since I really had no idea where it was. With Darius sleeping, I could probably sneak away and get Yipes to help me. But then, how much did I really know about Yipes? I reasoned not much more than I knew about Darius. Still, I felt sure Yipes would help me if I ran back to him.

I paced back and forth in front of the hole, unsure of what I should do.

"You were chosen for other reasons as well." It was Darius, his head up and alert now, and his piercing dark eyes staring at me. "We have been watching you with interest for quite some time. You plot and scheme in search of a way outside the wall. You have always known there was a higher purpose for your life, some mysterious duty, maybe even a mysterious past you can't remember. Your searching has not been as aimless as you might think." Darius rose and took four ominous strides towards me. I imagined he could stand his own against any man or beast I knew of.

"Do you know where the rock in the pool came from, and why it allows you to understand what I'm saying? Have you any idea what happened to Renny Warvold? Who is this Elyon and where is he? I think the answers to these questions, and many more, would surprise you. But first things first—you won't understand why we brought you here until you go down that dark hole and see for yourself.

"Your adventure begins or ends here, Alexa."

I hesitated for a moment longer, taking in a big breath of the fresh mountain air and looking up into the light blue of the morning sky. Leaves danced in the wind; a hawk circled overhead. I wondered if Yipes had sent it to watch over me.

I got down on all fours and poked my head into the hole, knowing already that I would soon find myself deep under the earth; unable to resist the temptation of discovery Darius had so aptly placed in front of me.

My hands were next. Touching the cool floor sent a rush of dirt rolling down into the shadows. My shoulders in, I could not turn back to look behind me without knocking loose dirt off the walls to my left or my right. It was claustrophobic, much smaller than it had looked. My body blocked what little of the sun's rays had been streaming into the hole, and only a few shards of light poorly illuminated the space in front of me. With my knees inside I encountered an additional discomfort. The hunch of my back bumped against the top of the tunnel as I waddled from side to side. I could get my front half down by bending my elbows, but my rear end was a protruding mass that was hard to control in the tight underground space; keeping it down required me to bend back on my ankles and move forward in short, awkward shuffles. When I was all the way in and only a few feet down the hole, a cold, dry darkness surrounded me.

How far did Darius say it was? A hundred feet, a hundred yards? I could not remember, but whatever the distance I was sure it would seem like a hundred miles. The further I shuffled in, the darker it seemed. After a while, I closed my eyes to keep the dirt from stinging them. Within twenty minutes, my back and knees began to ache, and a horrible fear gripped me. I opened my eyes and had the strange effect of a dream from which I could not wake; blackness turned to blackness as I opened and shut my eyes, and a dark terror welled up in my throat.

It occurred to me at that moment that I could not turn around. Would not, in fact, be able to turn around when it came time to retreat out of the tunnel. Shuffling forward was hard enough, but backwards would be impossible. I would die underground, exhausted and bawling in the end, probably wedged sideways in an ill-fated attempt to turn around. I began to hyperventilate and see a rainbow of colored stars in the darkness. Another moment and I was sure I would pass out with my face in the dirt.

I leaned back on my ankles and tried to calm down. *Twenty minutes in. Why hadn't I counted each of my shuffles forward?* If each of my advances were a foot in length, then I was moving at a rate of twenty feet per minute, which would put me four hundred feet into the tunnel. That would mean Darius was lying, since I had already gone at least a hundred yards. He had probably already covered the entryway with dirt and wandered off into the woods looking for a hapless victim he could devour for lunch. I lay down on my belly against the cold black dirt of my tomb, unsure what to do next.

I knew I could not turn around or go backwards all the way out. I reasoned that the only choices I had were to keep going forward or lie where I was and starve to death. Three shuffles into my decision to go on, my hand encountered air where it should have found floor.

I lowered onto my belly again and tried to reach down and feel the bottom with both arms dangling, but it was too far down to touch. The walls to the sides were also gone, and I perceived a faint light creeping into the space. I took a pebble and dropped it over the edge and heard it pop at the bottom a few feet below. I slithered down into the new open space like a dry snake and found I could stand.

Maybe Darius had only been bad with distance, not bad altogether.

I felt around for walls and found open air all around me for several paces. Then I reached a wall that was clearly made of wood planks, and I felt along its surface to the ceiling a foot above my head. The faint glow I had discerned earlier was not enough to illuminate the darkness, but the sliver of light it created was clear against the grain of the wood. A small opening, no more than an inch, poured a weak beam of dusty light.

I stood with my back against one of the walls and stared at the sliver of light. As I approached the wall and placed my one eye over the small opening, I could not imagine what I might see on the other side.

It was a room. A lamp hung on the far wall, and another to my right, from which I could only see light glittering here and there. A table and two chairs, a map on the facing wall with locations I had never seen winding in a yarn of twists and turns of brown and black. It was a dimly lit room with earth walls, and I could not see from where it might be entered.

I heard voices, distant echo's at first, like sounds from the meeting room at Renny Lodge when I tried to listen from outside closed doors as my father warned me not to do. I had that same heart-racing fear as the voices came closer. It was two men, arguing about something, and as they approached, their words became clearer, a muffled language I knew well.

"I don't care about what he says, we've waited far too long already," said the first man.

"I know you want to go, a lot of us do. What do you want *me* to do about it? He'll go when he's good and ready to go," said the other man. They were in the room now, to my left out of my direct sight, but close.

"Why can't we schedule a meeting so we can tell him we need to get on with it?" said the first man.

They passed in front of me, and I jerked away from the hole with a yelp, falling backwards with a dull, earthy thud. I was afraid they might have heard me, and I cringed at the thought of seeing another eye staring back at me through the hole, the boards flying in great splinters as they broke through and discovered my hiding place. Soft light was still finding its way through the tiny opening, and the voices moved a little farther away. I silently positioned my eye to the hole, and saw that they had settled at the desk to continue their discussion as they reviewed the map hanging above them on the wall. Their tone was quieter and with the added distance I was allowed only a word here or a fragment there. "Too long," "I understand," an emphatic "No!" Most of what I heard was a garble of useless words I could not tie together into any meaning.

The light was soft and I only saw silhouettes of the men against the wall. They were dressed plainly; both had beards and were good sized. Based on their voices I put them at middle age.

One of the men rose from the desk and began walking toward me, apparently to retrieve something from my side of the room. He was a big man, and as he approached I could see his hair was unkempt and his beard overgrown. His clothes were ragged. He came closer still, almost right in front of me. He struck a matchstick and lit another lamp that hung just to the right of the opening I was looking through. As the light flickered to life, I saw without a doubt what Darius had sent me to see.

This ragged looking man had an 'S' branded squarely on his forehead.

THE FOREST COUNCIL

It took me half as long to get out of the tunnel as it had taken me to crawl all the way in. The trip out was much harder on my body as I bumped my elbows, knees, and back in a race for the exit. When I emerged from the hole, the light and heat hit me with its full force, and it took me several seconds to see anything but sheets of flaming white and yellow. I was exhausted and lay on my back, hands over my eyes, listening to the wind rushing through the leaves on the trees.

"You must be hungry. How about we open up that bag of yours and have something to eat?" It was Darius. He stood a few feet away. I rolled over on my side and looked at him through narrowed eyes. "What are those men doing down there? I saw one of them up close; he had an 'S' branded on his forehead. Do you have any idea what that means?" I said.

"Oh, I know precisely what it means young lady, and so will you shortly. But first some lunch, shall we?"

I gave Darius some dried meat and it was gone in a flash of teeth and slaver. I chomped indifferently on bread as we walked, slowly making our way back in the direction of the Lathbury wall that divided the mountains from the forest. I kept questioning Darius about the men I had seen, but he seemed content to quietly continue on, winding his way through thick underbrush and around the occasional fallen tree. Finally, in frustration, I yelled at him, "Can't you just stop for a minute and tell me *something?*"

Darius did stop and turned back at me. "I am responsible for two things today: getting you down that hole and having you in Malcolm's capable hands by midday. So far, I've accomplished only one of those tasks. All of your questions will be answered before the sun sets tonight, but for now, I can't tell you anything more." He turned and started walking again, and though I felt completely exasperated I followed, trailing a few feet behind him down the path.

It was a long, hot journey, but at midday we were standing in a grove of cottonwood trees fifty yards from the Lathbury wall. The gate to Bridewell was now safely in the distance and looking overhead I could see that several hawks were patrolling the area from above, dodging a storm of white floating fluff from the trees. As I stood catching my breath with Darius, I saw rustling under the brush in the distance, a zing of gray, then more rustling.

"Ah, here he comes. Not much good for sleuthing, but a nice fellow still the same," said Darius. We watched as the formless gray ball of fir continued to weave in and out of view. After a while it became clear that it was a rabbit darting toward us between hiding places in the undergrowth. It was taking quite a long time for him to find his way to us.

"Will you *please* stop with the secret spy routine and get over here!" cried Darius. "You'll make us all late." For a moment there was no movement at all.

"Is that you, Darius?" came a tiny, uncertain voice from somewhere in the thicket.

"Yes it's me, the big wolf come to eat the helpless bunny. The longer you take getting over here the hungrier I get," said Darius.

A gray head topped with floppy ears popped up about twenty yards away. "Coming!" said the rabbit with great exuberance, and he was standing at my feet a few seconds later.

"No need to get hostile," said the rabbit, which I took to be Malcolm. "Ah, but I see you've got the girl, and on time. Nicely done."

"All in a days work for a lonely bachelor," said Darius, and then he became quiet and looked at Malcolm with a terrible sadness. "Have you any word from Odessa and Sherwin?"

"Stop your pouting, it's pathetic for a creature of your size. This will all be over before you know it Darius, trust me," said Malcolm. "Now, how about a proper introduction?"

Darius growled and then introduced me. Malcolm held out his foot in an effort to shake my hand. He said it was human custom to shake, and he wanted to make me feel at home. I bent down, took his furry gray foot between my thumb and forefinger, and awkwardly bobbed it up and down a few times. Malcolm chuckled nervously and we both looked at Darius who rolled his eyes. I laughed, and for the first time I felt a little less like a guest outside the wall, a little more like these might actually be my friends.

Darius and Malcolm huddled together and talked while I relieved myself behind a tree. This produced a whole new conversation about when to go to the bathroom, where to go to the bathroom, and whether or not one should cover up when they were finished.

After several minutes of arguing, Darius said, "I suggest we continue this conversation when we have more time. Though I will concede Malcolm's views on marking trees over rocks makes a compelling argument."

Malcolm looked up at me and I nodded my readiness to move on.

"I'll go straight to see Yipes and tell him of our progress. He will be pleased to hear you've come this far," said Darius. Then, with a slight bow of his head, he added, "Malcolm, always a great pleasure. Take care of our girl now, and tell everyone I'm doing fine." Then he walked off, and I was left with nothing but a smiling ball of fur with poor scouting skills to protect me. I felt suddenly alone and I missed my father and friends back in Bridewell. I think I even missed Pervis, or maybe I missed the morbid comfort of his rude behavior.

"You've grown some from what I was told about your size. It must have been quite a squeeze getting down that tunnel over at Lunenburg," said Malcolm. "The next one's not so bad."

"The *next* one?" I said.

"Sure the next one. Didn't Darius tell you? We've got a big meeting over in the forest tonight. Lots to discuss."

We walked, or I should say, I walked and Malcolm hopped, towards the Lathbury wall. Tucked down in the underbrush was another hole, and Malcolm easily fit inside. I followed and found that it was indeed a bit roomier, but not by much. I was barely able to stay up on my knees without bumping my back against the top, and it was just as narrow as the previous tunnel from side to side, so I continually grazed my shoulders and elbows along the walls. This tunnel descended faster, leveled out, and then began to rise again, presumably on the other side of the wall. Pretty soon I saw light streaming down, and shortly after that we were outside again, only now we were at the break between the mountain and the forest on the other side of the Lathbury wall.

"Who are Odessa and Sherwin?" I asked, turning my head to the side and shaking the dirt out of my hair.

Malcolm didn't answer at first, but then he stopped hopping and looked at me. "Odessa is Darius's wife, and Sherwin is his son," he said.

"Darius was off hunting for several weeks. They put the wall up so fast, and there were so many humans about, he got caught on the mountain side. He hasn't seen his family in quite some time."

I thought a moment, trying to consider the consequences of what Malcolm had said.

"Are there other stories like his?" I asked.

He turned on the path and began hopping again, his floppy back feet kicking up tiny storms of dust as he went. "more than a few," he said.

We continued to make our way deeper into the woods. It was turning dark and cooling down. The forest was vastly different from where I had just spent two days. The mountain region had been far more open and arid, with tiny streams crisscrossing and connecting all over. Twenty minutes into our walk away from the wall put us deep in a forest of fir, pine, cottonwood, and aspen trees. The lush forest floor was alive and danced with shadows cast from an endless parade of swaying trees. As we approached early evening it was cool and peaceful, the sound of the trees moving in the wind high above seemed like a friendly traveling companion, calling us deeper and deeper into the depths of the forest.

As we walked, I kept thinking about the face of that haggard man with the 'S' on his forehead. It must have stung something awful when he was branded. I guess Warvold could be cruel now that I thought about it. How these men had escaped into The Dark Hills remained a biting question I couldn't get out of my mind.

I began to feel a creepy sense that we were being watched and I started hearing what sounded like whispers all around me. I kept shaking the cobwebs loose from my head trying to refocus, but the strange whispering sound persisted, and I reasoned that it was the wind in the trees playing tricks on me.

"Malcolm, do you hear anything strange?" I said.

Malcolm stopped and sniffed at the air with his front legs up. "Oh yes, we've got quite a procession going already. You're famous, Alexa. Every animal within twenty miles is hiding behind a bush or a tree limb trying to get a peek at you." Things were getting stranger all the time.

We wound through the forest for another five minutes and then came to a stop where the trail split off into two directions, one straight ahead and one veering off to the left and down towards the Lunenburg wall; both were covered by a thick canopy of low hanging tree branches.

"It looks like we've arrived, Alexa. Go on now, go straight ahead up that trail and don't stop until you see Ander."

"What's an Ander?" I asked.

"You mean *who* is Ander," chortled Malcolm. "Go on then—you'll get all your questions answered once you reach the end of that path."

I did as I was told, too tired to complain or argue with a rabbit. A few minutes later the path widened into a circular area about forty feet around bordered by large rocks and dead tree trunks. The rocks and trees were covered with animals, more animals than I had ever seen before—squirrels, rabbits, mountain lions, bears, wolves, beavers, badgers, porcupines, skunks, and a smattering of wildlife I could not identify from my own limited knowledge. It was a frightening sight, made worse by the swarm of whispering I continued to hear buzzing in my head.

Straight ahead, right up the middle of all the animals, was a ferocious looking grizzly bear. Its head was like a boulder on its massive shoulders, and it swayed back and forth as the beast walked towards me. The whispering stopped. I was about to turn and run for my life when I spotted Yipes sitting on a rock to my right. I was so happy to see him again; I couldn't help the big smile on my worn-out face. I read his lips as he mouthed the words, "It's okay, stay calm."

The grizzly stopped close enough in front of me that its wet nostrils sent a gentle wind through my hair. I looked down and saw where its enormous paws smashed the mossy green grass at my feet. It stood still on four legs, its head a foot above my own. I knew from what I had read about Grizzly bears that one quick swipe from his paw would break my bones and shred my skin. I stood perfectly still, breathing in and out in choppy waves.

"We have waited for you a long, long time my dear," said the Grizzly. His voice was deep, sorrowful, and slow. He seemed old, though I had no idea how old by the looks of him. "I am Ander, the forest king, and I have a lot to tell you.

"Bring the food!" he said, and a parade of animals came out of the woods with offerings of nuts, fruits, and fresh water.

"Now, let's sit down and have a nice long chat shall we, Alexa?" said Ander.

We walked to the center of the grove and sat down. I drank until I thought I would throw up, and then I pulled some left over meat out of my bag to eat with the nuts and the fruit.

"If you don't mind, Alexa, could you get by without the meat for now? Mixed company you know, it sets them off," said Ander, and he looked around at all the animals. They were all staring at me with wide eyes, and some of the larger animals were dripping saliva and acting strange.

I put my food away and began eating a pear, which suited me fine. Ander proceeded to introduce me to a number of important animals in attendance.

I met Murphy, a lively squirrel who kept zipping back and forth and twirling around in circles after his name was called. It took a while to get him calmed down, and he continued doing back flips and whirling spins every time Ander introduced another animal. There was Beaker, a raccoon. Ander said he was "scientific for a coon, a problem solver." A badger named Henry was complimented on his fierce fighting skills. Picardy was a beautiful female black bear that had not seen her mate in a very long time; he had been off in the mountains looking for a den when the wall came tumbling into existence. I met Boone, a crafty bobcat, who often came up with outlandish ideas that, for some unknown reason, actually worked most of the time. There was a quick and sneaky fox named Raymond, and a woodchuck named Vesper. Chopper and Whip were an agreeable pair of buck-toothed beavers.

The sun was beginning to set and I was getting cold. It must have shown, because Ander took a break from his introductions to call Yipes over, who presented me with a blanket out of his pack. I draped it around my shoulders and curled my legs up to my chest, wrapping my arms around my knees. Soon it would be night, but for now dusk coated the grove with a soft blend of velvety gold and green. It was heavenly.

Ander finished the introductions with Odessa and Sherwin, the wife and son of Darius. Sherwin approached me cautiously, swaying his head back and forth. He was every bit the powerful beast his father was, but his features were more juvenile and his coat was a lighter shade of gray.

"You've met my father?" he questioned me.

"Yes, I've met Darius. He's impressive," I said. I felt a wave of compassion for Sherwin, wondering what it must be like to lose your father in such an unjust way. I added, "When did you last see him?"

"I don't remember ever seeing him. I was only a few months old when he was caught behind the wall. When I was smaller and I could fit through the tunnel, I thought many times about sneaking under to find him. Now I'm so big I can barely squeeze through the hole. Anyway, walking deep into a long, dark tunnel, that's something I just can't do. A den is one thing; a tight little tunnel in which I cannot turn around is something all together different. It would be something like you trying to fly; it's not in your range of abilities, you're not equipped for the task. For many of us here, size is only the obvious reason we cannot chase after a loved one. The greater, and more mysterious reason is our inability to bring ourselves to do it. We know not the reasons why Elyon makes us the way he does, but we are stuck with what he gives us."

He paused and looked off towards the Lathbury wall in the distance.

"At night, my father howls at me, and I howl back at him.

We dream of hunting together and of he and my mother being side by side again. He often sounds sad, and in recent times, even a little old, like the long lonely nights are beginning to wear on him. Sometimes he howls at me for hours and hours, until his voice is shredded and crackling. On those nights I often go to the hole that leads under the wall and I put my front paws in, and I imagine I'm small again. Then I look to the wall and beat my head against the same spot until blood is oozing out of my fur and into my eyes.

"My story is not so different than what many of these animals here would tell you. Most of the large animals have lost a son or daughter, a mate, a close friend or a parent. Others feel the terrible loss of the mountains and the lush, wild streams lined with fruit trees and blackberry patches. The smaller animals, the ones who can use the tunnels, those have maintained a relatively normal life after the walls," Sherwin said.

"What makes you think dragging me out here will make any difference?" I said. "I'm only a child, and I command no special importance in Bridewell. I create more bad than good back there, ask anyone."

Sherwin looked down for a long moment, then straight into my eyes with a heartbreaking look on his face. "Then we have clearly chosen wrong, and we should send you back. You're small enough to use the tunnels and you have the right breeding, those things are true. What you lack is *belief*. If bringing down the wall would require you to fly, you must believe that you can fly. Otherwise, when the decisive moment comes, you will surely discover you have no wings."

He turned and walked back to stand at his mother's side. The whispers and the sun were both gone. The sounds of owls, crickets, and frogs blended together to form a thick soup of mystifying night music. The full moon rose out of the trees from the east, pouring a bucket of soft white into the grove. And again I felt the discomforting loneliness that so often haunted me.

"I see you've got quite a scratch there on your arm," said Ander, his deep voice jerking me out of my self-pity. "I do apologize. Domesticated animals can be rather pesky at times. That's not to say Sam and Pepper are bad cats, they've actually been helpful in our attempts to get you out here. But they can be, shall we say, *spirited*.

"Now then, I believe you have a stone in your possession, which I must now ask you to produce. That is, if you don't mind," said Ander. "It may be that you are not the person for the job at hand, even if I'm quite convinced that you are. In any case, the stone will tell us a lot about what your future holds."

With all that was going on I had completely forgotten about the stone hanging around my neck in the small leather pouch. I clutched it under the blanket, afraid at first to give it up; afraid I might never get it back. I wiggled open the string at the top, and removed the stone. When I held it out to Ander, the feathery green glow illuminated the space between the two of us, and the crowd of animals let out a meandering collection of oohs and ahs. I set the stone down on a large flat rock that sat between us, and it continued to throb liquid green light like the steady time of a beating drum. *Boom, boom, boom.*

"Beautiful, isn't it?" said Ander, as he gazed at its strange throbbing radiance. *Boom, boom, boom.*

"This entire area including the forest, mountains, and hills, was at one time full of Elyon's enchantment. It was a marvelous place indeed. The stone you chose is what allows you to communicate with us, just as we communicate with each other.

"At one time there were six stones like this one in the pool. Yipes found the first, then another was taken, then the slaves came and took all but this one." He nodded towards the pulsating green mass sitting between us. "In these stones lie the answer to why Elyon created us, why he created this place, and where he's gone off to."

Ander sat silent then for a long time, his heavy breathing filled the air, and it seemed as though he were praying to an unseen god, searching for something in the silence he couldn't quite find. And then he came back to life again.

"Unfortunately, we haven't the time to talk about all that right now," he said. "Elyon is on the move, his plans are unfolding in this very age, and we shall all be a witness to his triumphant return in the days to come. One thing I can tell you; someone you once knew was responsible for bringing the stones here, but that is about all we have time for."

"Thomas Warvold," I said, without the slightest hesitation.

"An excellent guess. He is responsible for a great many things that, in his death, we are all left to consider. But he did not bring the stones. They were placed in the pool by his wife, Renny."

Ander looked at the sky and sniffed at the air, then continued.

"When things settle down you can come see me again and I'll tell you all about the mysterious Warvolds. For now, we really must be getting on with things."

I started to protest. I asked about Elyon, whom I had never thought of as more than a legend. I asked about another man I'd heard mention of, Blackwell, who he was and where he could be found. But at every turn Ander insisted we stay on his choice of topics, that the time for those answers had not yet come. I wasn't about to have it out with a thousand pound Grizzly, but his comments left me terribly curious to learn more about Thomas, Renny, and in particular Elyon.

"All magic runs out sometime Alexa, and this place has been running out for some time now. We used to be able to communicate with the birds; now they understand us but we do not understand them. We can send them off to do things, but we cannot be sure if they have done what we asked them to. Oh, they can tell us a little by the way they move or the sounds they make. But it's as if we speak completely different languages now.

"Some of the animals are beginning to experience the same problems," Ander continued. "We can comprehend each other most of the time, but occasionally our voices become garbled for a morning or an afternoon, only to return again some hours later. This process accelerated after the wall went up."

Ander touched the stone with the edge of his paw and gently pushed it two or three inches along the flat rock. The fluid green light continued to pulsate between the two of us.

"With humans, the stone gives you two important things," he continued, putting his paw back on the ground. "The ability to communicate with animals and a glimpse into the future. In other words, it gives new insight in two ways: present and future. Just like any magical effect, this one comes with its own set of rules. For instance, the ability to talk with animals only works if you stay in the wild. As soon as you leave, the power begins to drift away. Once this process starts it cannot be reversed, and there are no more stones to be had. Once you leave the wild, the stone will start its gradual descent into dim regularity. It will throb more slowly, and with less intensity, over a period of undetermined time.

"As you can probably imagine, Yipes has never left the wild of the forest and the mountains, and so he continues to enjoy the questionable benefits of speaking with animals." Ander took a moment to look over at Yipes with a nod and a wink, and then he continued.

"I said before that a stone was taken by someone other than Yipes or the slaves. That person set a stone right where you've just set yours, and it glowed like a small but glorious orange sun at the tail end of a hot day. Can you guess who might have sat where you sit now, Alexa?" Said Ander.

I thought for a moment about the possible answers to

the question, but I was sure I knew whom Ander was talking about.

"Warvold," I said.

"Absolutely! It was none other than Mr. Warvold himself, the great adventurer. Would you like to hear what his stone revealed about his future?"

I nodded yes and he leaned forward over the table, the green glow from my stone wafting through his bushy fur with a watery glow.

"Warvold's stone revealed that one day terrible forces from this enchanted land would rise up and cause the destruction of everything he had created," said Ander.

"Warvold took this to mean that some sort of dark monsters lived out here that would someday enter his kingdom and kill everyone. But he badly misread the meaning of his future."

"He was mistaken, just like he told me," I interjected. "He told me he'd gotten it all wrong when he sat with me that last night with our backs against the wall." My head was reeling as I tried to put it all together. "His future wasn't about dark enchanted monsters at all. He made his own monsters, then let them loose in The Dark Hills to—"

"Now don't get too far ahead of yourself, Alexa, you're only half right. Allow me the indulgence of giving you the whole story, if you would," said Ander. "When Warvold was told about his future he was terrified for his wife Renny and all the people streaming into Lunenburg. He was beside himself with grief. We tried to explain to him that the Jocasta could be misinterpreted to mean something it did not, and we assured him that we knew of no evil monsters lurking about."

"Did you say Jocasta?" I said.

"Yes. That's what the messages etched on the stones are called," said Ander.

"How much did Renny Warvold have to do with all this?" I said.

"A lot, and she was smarter than you can imagine. She brought the enchanted stones here. She started everything." Ander hunched his enormous back up and let out a low rumbling growl.

"I'm not as young as I once was, and we're approaching my bedtime," he said absentmindedly. "Where was I? Oh yes, when Warvold returned to Lunenburg he hatched a plan to build a wall before any further expansion. He added more guards and made the arrangement with the leaders in Ainsworth. Everything went as planned, and during the span of the next several years Warvold completed not one but three walled roads, along with three new principalities. By the time he'd gone this far he'd figured out how to use 300 slaves and hundreds more of his own men to build quickly. The wall between the forest and the mountains was the last. First he built it only eight feet high, then his own people followed behind to finish the rest. It was remarkable really, sometimes a thousand feet a day were walled in, quickly cutting off the passage between the forest and the mountains. By all accounts the operation was a marvel of speed and efficiency.

"But Warvold made one important miscalculation in his plan: He trusted the leaders in Ainsworth to take back the prisoners. Further, he took them at their word when they said they indeed had taken them back. You see, until that night when you sat with him, Warvold never knew that the leaders in Ainsworth had set those men free in The Dark Hills. They never thought Warvold would actually give them back, and they had planned poorly for the return of the prisoners. The officials in Ainsworth had no place to put them, and so they delivered them into The Dark Hills and banished them to the caves. The way the Ainsworth officials figured it, nobody would ever be the wiser."

"What caves are you talking about, Ander? I never heard of any caves out there," I said.

"The caves that were formed when all the materials for the wall were dug up, of course. My dear, there are miles of giant tunnels out there in The Dark Hills, and miles more on the surface made of thick, thorny underbrush. That's how the prisoners get around both above and below ground without being seen. Where do you think almost three hundred men are going to go?

"Those walls, those miles and miles of walls, are made from a clay that could only be found underground. Clay is a plentiful substance out there in The Dark Hills, and easy to harvest. All one has to do is dig a few feet under the ground and start tunneling. Everything in the tunnel's path will be pure clay, which was the primary ingredient Warvold wanted for the building blocks.

"It really isn't all Warvold's fault things have developed as they have. Nonetheless, it was his fear that drove him to create a monster. The monster he created is not the collection of prisoners who live in The Dark Hills. The monster is the wall itself. But I suppose that would be a debate for another time, now wouldn't it?"

Everything was becoming clear now. It was like a giant puzzle with interlocking pieces, and Ander had just fit everything together on one moonlit evening. Only it seemed in the telling that one piece was left missing.

"Ander, why am I out here?" I said.

The whispers started up again, and Murphy did back flips and spins. It was exhausting to watch the little squirrel expend so much energy. Ander lifted his head up and the grove went still and quiet again.

"We believe that Warvold's death set in motion the beginning of the end of this age. We have no idea if this eventual end will take five days or five years, but we know it is coming. For better or for worse, you are the chosen one, and not just by us, but by Warvold himself. There is just a tad more I must tell you now, and then we really must get on with reading your stone and shuffling you off to bed. It's getting late, very late indeed.

"Alexa, all that you are being told must be kept a secret until the time is right to reveal what you know. Someone is not what they seem in Bridewell. That someone is the one the prisoners call Sebastian. He is living inside Bridewell, giving the orders, making things ready for a time when the prisoners will invade all of Bridewell and bring Warvold's future to pass. Who is Sebastian? I'm sure the birds could tell us if we could understand them, but we have no idea. None whatsoever. I can tell you but one thing. The slaves left the last stone for a reason. They meant it for their leader, and when they find it has been taken, it will enrage them even more.

"Sebastian must be found out and revealed for the serpent that he is, and the prisoners must be stopped from invading Bridewell. Cut off the serpent's head, and the whole serpent dies. The prisoners are not brilliant men, Alexa. However, they are extremely vengeful, and Sebastian *is* brilliant. At present, this is a lethal combination.

"If power is transferred to the slaves war will be upon us, and the wall will become a military stronghold. Once set in motion, violence will reign down on Bridewell and the wall will remain, possibly forever. We must reveal and remove the danger, and in so doing convince people that the danger is past. That's our only hope of bringing down the wall." Ander was skirting around the point he was trying to make, then he stammered and got right to the heart of the matter.

"You cannot tell anyone about what has taken place here tonight. *Especially* about Sebastian," he said.

"You think Sebastian might be my own father?" I said. The remark was met with a cold, silent stare from Ander. "I know my father, and he's no former slave working against our people," I yelled. But even in saying it, I knew I could not know for sure.

"We can't be certain that Sebastian was a slave," Ander continued. "It could be someone on the inside who knows more than they are telling and has a motive to side with them. Perhaps it's someone looking for more power, like a disgruntled son or a crafty guard with wicked ambitions. Maybe it's an old man who fixes books, or a simple mail carrier with timely access to powerful people. It could be anyone. That is why you can't tell what you know. It's also one more reason Warvold chose you. You know how to work alone and maintain secrecy. You're small and easily hidden. You have connections to important people, but you're not important enough yourself to be scrutinized too closely. Face it Alexa, you're perfect for the task."

I couldn't argue with Ander's reasoning.

"Only one thing left to do; read your Jocasta," said Ander.

"What if I don't want it revealed? What if I'd rather not know my future?" I said.

"That is your choice to make and we will honor it. But in this case, I must say, I think your Jocasta will give you much needed clarity for the days to come," said Ander.

I sat silent for a long moment, and then I looked straight into the grizzly's powerful face.

"Read it," I said.

Yipes jumped down off his perch and walked towards us. He crawled right up on the big flat rock and removed a magnifying glass from his vest. Then he held the glass against his eye, and put his face less than an inch from the rhythmically pulsating stone. *Boom, boom, boom goes the slow beating drum.* After a moment, he rose into a sitting position and looked at Ander. Ander nodded and Yipes looked at me.

"You shall cut off the serpent's head," he said.

I guess that was that.

PART 2

An Unexpected Enemy

The trap door wavered in the air while Yipes held it up as best he could, but the door was heavy and well over twice his height. I think he pretended to make it look more difficult than it was so he could more easily avoid eye contact with me. We were both sad that I was going back to Bridewell this morning.

"You have a visitor, Alexa," said Yipes. I looked back over my shoulder into the heat of the morning sun. Standing motionless off in the distance was the silhouette of a large wolf. I waved to him and he turned to the west and headed up into the mountains.

"I've got to go," I said.

I started down the ladder into the dark tunnel. "Wait!" yelled Yipes. "I almost forgot to give you this." He reached into his vest pocket and pulled out a small tube. "Not to be shared until *you know who* is found out. And one other thing," he wagged his finger at me, trying to balance the heavy door with his other hand. "Be careful who you talk to from here on out. Trust *no one*." As he said this it was clear he was losing control of the trap door, and it swayed ominously above me. I scrambled down another three rungs as fast as I could and the door came swinging down on top of the hole with its full force, slamming down and showering me with a storm of dirt.

I lost my grip with one arm and hung by three fingers from a rung of the ladder. A few more inches and the door would have hammered me like a nail into a thirty-foot freefall.

I regained my footing and my grip on the ladder and shook the dirt from my hair and shoulders. It was pitch black in the tunnel. I waited and waited for Yipes to open the door, but it remained dark and quiet. "Yipes!" I yelled, but received no answer. I removed a wooden match from my pouch and struck it against the ladder. The light revealed the lamp I had left hanging on the third rung down. Thankfully it had not plunged to the floor and smashed into useless pieces.

I lit the lamp and felt much better once I could see my surroundings. I held it out over the open air, but I could not see the bottom. The darkness swallowed up the light about ten feet down. I waited until the intense pain in my hands threatened my grip on the ladder. I called again for Yipes but got no answer. Then I started the slow descent to the floor of the tunnel, moving the lamp down three rungs at a time as I went.

When I reached the bottom I found the book I had left behind, covered in dirt. Cabeza de Vaca, the cow head. "I bet you never thought you'd see me again. You're looking well these days. Travels treating you all right?" A sparkle from the corner of the tunnel caught my eye and I held the lamp over it. There in the dirt was the tube Yipes had given me. It was about four inches long and an inch around, with jewels imbedded across its wood surface. The top was closed with a wooden cork.

I removed the cork with a pop and took out a paper scroll. Attached was a note, which read 'make sure you don't accidentally give this to the wrong person,' and it was signed by Yipes. I unrolled the paper and revealed what looked to be an exact copy of the map I had seen hanging on the wall in the tunnel where the men were. This must have been what Yipes was working on when he spent time down in that secret passageway.

The map showed both black and brown lines, along with

notations about some of them. The black lines represented below ground tunnels, the brown ones above ground passage-ways created by thick brush. I'd have to give the map careful review when I had more light, and make sure it didn't fall into the wrong hands.

I looked up once more, hoping I would see a crack of light and Yipes' little face peering down at me. Seeing only darkness, I turned and started walking for Bridewell. My pace quick-ened when I thought of seeing my father, Grayson, Ganesh, Nicolas, and Silas. I slowed down when I thought of Pervis. The thought of sleeping in my own bed or talking to Sam and Pepper for the first time or searching for a good book in the library got me moving faster again. Knowing that the second I opened the trap door back into the library my stone would start weakening and my ability to talk with the animals would slowly disappear made me shuffle slowly and look over my shoulder in the direction I'd come from. It was a bittersweet journey to say the least.

My thoughts kept returning to Elyon and all that Ander had said about him. The mystery of this mythical 'creator' had drifted into my head and I couldn't get it out. My world had always been so small, hidden behind walls. I was beginning to think this 'Land of Elyon' was bigger and more dangerous than anything I could have imagined. How many more mysteries were waiting for me beyond the walls?

Eventually I stood on the ladder at the top of the tunnel in the stairwell, listening for any sign of movement in the library. It seemed to me that I had been gone a lifetime, seen a whole new world, and returned as an all-together different person.

"Is that you, Alexa?" came a feline voice from the other side.

Be careful who you talk to from here on out. Trust no one. Yipes' words clanged around in my head like a dinner bell.

"It's me, Sam," came the cat's voice again. It was strange

to understand his meowing, but its meaning was crystal clear. "Pepper is keeping an eye on Grayson. It's all clear for you to come out," he said.

I opened the trap door toward me, blew out the lamp and hung it on a rung, and then pushed the chair out of the way. The light was bright at first and I only saw the silhouette of Sam looking down at me from his roost on the back of the chair. I smiled and said, "Hey Sam! How are you doing?"

"Alexa, answer me. Can you understand what I'm saying, Alexa?" said Sam, his dark outline held motionless against the dusty light streaming in behind him.

"Come on Alexa, let's have it! I know you can understand me. I want to hear the latest from Ander," said Sam.

Sam jumped down and leaned against my legs, staring up at me with his penetrating gray eyes. Time seemed to stand still as he purred and paced back and forth. He took a final, long look at me, and then jumped back up on the chair.

"Stupid girl," he said. "As useless as ever. All you hear is purring and meowing all the livelong day. I should have expected as much." I turned away from Sam toward the bookshelf and fanned my hands over the rows of books to hide the shock on my face.

"Go! Tell Sebastian she has returned as weak and worthless as ever," he said. The command sent a flash of shadows around the room and the sound of wings beating against glass. I had not noticed the perfectly still hawk sitting in the sill, listening, waiting for orders.

I tried desperately to remember all the things Sam and Pepper would have seen me doing or heard me saying. How many times had hawks watched me? Were they watching when Warvold died and I took the key? I absentmindedly ran my hand along my forearm, feeling the wicked scratch Pepper had given me when I'd tried to take his amulet in my hands. *Traitors, both of them.* I could hardly believe it. And the hawks, they were also traitors. I had to get a message to Ander.

"No more time for petting right now Sam, I've got lots to do." I moved the chair back into its proper place and dusted myself off as best I could. I was dirty, so sneaking up to my room for a quick clean up before anyone saw me was essential. I quietly wound my way through the corridors of books, creaking the floorboards here and there as I continued cautiously in the direction of Grayson's office. I peeked around the last corner and saw that his door was ajar, Pepper's long tail flicking up and down at the floor. I had a momentary feeling of fear as Sam purred up against my leg unexpectedly.

"Pepper!" he said. "She's as dumb as a post, not a word out of her." Pepper's head came whipping around in the door jam.

"That you Sam?" came Grayson's voice. Things were getting complicated in a hurry and I'd only been back in Bridewell for a few minutes.

I crept down the hallway as quietly as I could, Sam held back in front of Grayson's door. "That's it, slink off to your room for a nice long nap," said Sam.

The floorboards creaked a few paces from the library door and I froze for a brief moment.

"Who's there?…Alexa, is that you?" It was Grayson, but I was safely on the other side of the door and out of sight a second later.

My room had never looked so wonderful. I hid my stone, the tube Yipes had given me, and the other trinkets I had been carrying around. I put on a fresh set of clothes and performed a healthy bit of primping on myself, then I flopped down on my bed and felt as though I could sleep for a month. I thought of all the events of the past three days and drifted off into dreams of talking animals and men with 'S's branded on their foreheads.

I awoke at midday, sweaty and hot. I had been dreaming of a hawk at my window. It was scratching and clawing to get in, and in my dream I let the bird in and it chased me around my room, landed on my head, and ripped chunks of my hair out with its monstrous claws. As I sat up in my bed, all wet and clammy from the heat and the awful dream, I heard scraping at the shutter. Was I still dreaming or had I actually awoke? I cautiously got out of bed.

Everything hurt and my feet felt as though they were walking on a bed of nails. As I hobbled over to the window, I realized that whatever was banging and scratching to get in was much smaller than a hawk, and it was scampering around from side to side outside the shutter. It could only be one animal: Murphy, the hyperactive squirrel from the grove. I swung the shutters open and he spilled into the room, bouncing from place to place, sniffing everything and whipping his tail from side to side.

"This is an unexpected surprise," I said.

He was behind my bed between the bathroom and the nightstand and I had to walk around the room to find him. "I think it would be best if we stayed away from the window. You never know who might be watching us," he said.

I lay down on my stomach and propped myself up at the elbows. It felt good to be off my feet. Murphy remained lively, darting under the bed, flying out with a leap and landing on my back, running down my legs and circling back.

"Murphy, if you can calm down a minute, I have news."

"What sort of news? Is it good or bad?"

"Well, to be honest, I think it's mostly bad," I said.

Murphy's cavorting had turned to twitching and quick jerks from side to side. Given his nature, I think it took more effort for him to stay still than to scuttle half crazed around the room.

"Let's have it then, no point putting off the inevitable," said Murphy. He closed his eyes tightly and turned his head slightly to the left, as if this would somehow soften the blow of whatever I was about to say.

I was getting sore on my elbows so I dropped down with

my chin on my hands. I was eye to eye with him, only a few inches between us, and for no apparent reason I whispered when I spoke. "Sam and Pepper are traitors. On top of that, I think the birds might be against us. I know for sure of at least one hawk that's working for Sebastian. I haven't had time to find out much else. Just getting to my room was an adventure in itself, and I've been sleeping most of the day."

Murphy looked stunned as his eyes squeaked back open. He was still for the first time since I'd met him. "That is bad news, now isn't it? We've had our suspicions about the birds, but Sam and Pepper? I can hardly believe it."

"Believe it," I said.

"Ander will want to know about this right away," said Murphy. "I suppose I should go and tell him."

He started to leave, then stopped. "Oh, I almost forgot, it was Yipes who sent me. He said to tell you he was sorry for slamming the door on your head. It made rather a loud noise when it came down, and he ran off into the trees to hide, afraid someone or something might have heard. By the time he came back to check, you were gone. He will be pleased to hear that you're not injured in any way."

Murphy bolted for the window. He was sitting in the sill by the time I had my wretched, sore body up to its knees, leaning over my bed.

"How's the stone looking?" he said from the sill.

"I haven't looked, but we're talking, so I guess it must still be all right."

"Best to keep an eye on it every few hours if you can," said Murphy. He was fidgeting back and forth, looking out the window and then back at me.

"It will be a shame to lose you. Maybe we'll get lucky and it won't wear out," said Murphy. And then, with a final back flip, he was gone.

Just as well, I had a busy afternoon planned.

Pervis Returns from Holiday

My first encounter with just about everyone occurred in the main dining area. I arrived shortly before dinner, and it was bustling as usual with activity. Servants were bringing out food for the buffet; meats, cheeses, fresh fruits and vegetables, most imported from Ainsworth and all on gorgeous white china. My father was the first to greet me as I pranced into the room.

"Alexa! How's my girl? We arrived only an hour ago." He embraced me, lifted me high off the floor, and whispered in my ear, "Let's have a little talk after dinner."

I gave him a reassuring nod and straightened my shirt when he put me down. "You must go to Turlock more often. It brings out your sentimental side."

My father amply countered, "I'm just happy to be back so I can give you all my washing. I was down to my last clean shirt."

"Poppycock! You missed our little lady as much as I did." It was Ganesh, pulling me close to his side and rubbing my head with the knuckles of his other hand. "Next time, we're taking you with us. Any excitement while we were gone?" asked Ganesh, releasing me and bending down on one knee so that we were eye to eye.

"I wandered around town looking for trouble, but I

couldn't find any, so I read a book about a man who had a head like a cow."

Ganesh laughed and looked over at Grayson. "What kind of books are you letting into our library these days?" Grayson replied with only a grunt and a shrug of his shoulders.

I made my way to the table of food. It all looked so good, I snatched a plate and filled it with fresh bread, blackberries, and apple slices. Grayson was holed up over the strawberries, plucking them out with a tiny fork one by one and popping them into his mouth.

"I haven't seen you much in your father's absence. Come to think of it, I haven't seen you at all." He looked around the room, and then whispered to me. "Let's keep that between you and me, shall we?" He put another strawberry in his mouth and continued talking while he chewed. "Say, did you stop by the library this morning? I had the strangest encounter with the cats, and someone was about the place but ran off."

"Not me. It must have been one of the students from downstairs playing a prank on you or trying to steal books," I said. I was getting far too comfortable with lying to everyone, and it bothered me. Was there ever a time when lying was a good thing? Without knowing whom I should trust and whom I should not, I couldn't just blurt out the whole adventure and hope Sebastian wasn't in the room. My father, Ganesh, Grayson, Nicolas, Silas, they were all here, and I could not conceive of any one of them being Sebastian. The only missing person was Pervis.

"Where's my favorite man in uniform, Mr. Kotcher?" I asked.

"Still on holiday in Ainsworth visiting friends. He's due back tonight though, so don't get too awfully excited," said Nicolas. He was looking as handsome as ever.

"Wait just one minute. You mean Pervis has friends?" I said.

"Apparently so," chuckled Nicolas. "Absence makes the heart grow fonder and all that. Move it along Grayson, I'd like at least one strawberry to garnish my plate with."

Grayson just kept on poking berries with his little fork and ignored Nicolas entirely.

We sat around the table and enjoyed a lovely dinner. I ate and ate and ate, my hunger satisfied for the first time in days. My body was much less sore now and my strength ebbed back to within range of normal.

I was seated next to Silas, who leaned over and whispered in my ear; "I must speak with you privately after dinner," he said.

I nodded my approval of the idea, but added, "My father first, then I'm yours."

"A game of chess after dinner, Alexa?" said Silas a few minutes later.

"Sorry, Silas, she's already promised me a stroll around Bridewell. Maybe after that," said my father.

I replied to Silas: "Yes, that would be nice, but I warn you, chess is my game. Father and I started playing when I was only three."

"Well then, maybe you won't mind playing me sometime, now that I'm back from visiting my chums." It was the familiar slippery voice of Pervis Kotcher, coming from the entryway where he had meandered in unnoticed. His face was smeared with an awful smirk, and he was advancing on the buffet with an annoying saunter. He was clearly drunk. "That is, if you're willing to *wager*. I only play chess when something of value is at stake. I find it adds a whole new dimension to an otherwise boring diversion." He was piling meat and potatoes enough for a family of four onto his plate.

"But enough about a silly game," he continued. "On to more important topics, shall we? Say for instance, the attitude over in Ainsworth toward Bridewell these days. Getting a bit hot under the collar around those parts now aren't they?" Pervis seated himself opposite my father at the end of the table, swaying to and fro, using his fork to poke and stab as he continued his tirade.

Ganesh interjected, "Pervis, we're in mixed company. I'm warning you—"

"Warning me to *what?* To keep my mouth shut about the discord you and the rest of the idiots running this place have caused with Ainsworth? Those people are ready to run this place over, and they've got plenty of manpower to do it."

"Pervis!" shouted my father, but he would not be stopped.

"I could give Ainsworth the keys to our beloved Bridewell with what I know, so you might start treating me with a little more respect."

Ganesh rose, standing over Pervis like a giant oak tree over a craning woodchuck. "That's it, Pervis. You just crossed over the line to a place from which you will never return." Six guards rounded the corner and positioned themselves around the room; one remained at each side of him.

"Hold on now, I was just running off at the mouth—really now, this is ridiculous. I can help you defend this place—really I can, I—" Two guards lifted Pervis out of his chair against his will. He kicked and screamed obscenities, flipping his plate of food into the air. Around and around the plate went, sending food everywhere, then smashing into bits against a pitcher of water on the table.

"Take him to a holding cell and search his room," said my father. It appeared that Pervis had overplayed his hand, but somehow the whole scene seemed wrong. Pervis certainly was out of line, but he wasn't anything more than a drunken buffoon returning from holiday. While it was true his behavior was beneath even him, he was hardly a threat in his current condition. Maybe Ganesh and my father had finally become so tired of his ranting they couldn't take another outburst. One thing was for sure, the animals were right. Warvold's death had sent things rapidly spinning out of control. A cyclone was building, and Bridewell was at its center.

After Pervis' crazed dinner antics I was ready to walk around town with my father and breathe some fresh air, although strangely enough, I felt a measure of discontent knowing our head guard was drunk and detained while everything swirled around Bridewell. If the slaves were to advance tonight, I'd want Pervis sober and at the main tower barking orders to his men. Unless, of course, he was Sebastian, in which case things were going rather well.

"What was that all about?" I started the conversation as we paced the cobblestone pathway along one of Bridewell's winding side streets.

"We've been talking about locking him up for a while now, Alexa. Ever since Warvold died, he's been *totally* impossible. We all thought—I mean Ganesh and Nicolas and I—we thought a few days away would calm him down. But showing up drunk and filling the room with all that rubbish was the last straw. We'll have to find a way to get by without him."

"You'll get no argument from me about Pervis, though I do worry about our safety with our head guard behind bars. Especially if what he said was true." The one man I loathed more than any other and I was practically advocating his release, strange how circumstances were having a way of changing the way I felt about people.

"He's just trying to stir up trouble. I can't tell you much about our dealing with Ainsworth. True, things have been somewhat tense with them. With Warvold passing they've tried to assert more control. But it's nothing we can't handle," said my father. He sounded confident that everything was fine, but given what I knew, it was not a comforting discord he was feeding me. I knew problems were afoot, bigger problems then even he was aware of.

"So you stayed out of trouble while I was gone? No trying to jump over the wall?"

Trust no one. But this was my father, how could I not trust him? "I stayed out of trouble like you asked, but now that you've returned, I really must get back to breaking things. I have a reputation to protect."

My father stopped walking and smiled while he rubbed his chin. He seemed exhausted from worry and lack of sleep. I felt sorry for him just then, which was something I had never felt for him before.

"Just be careful, all right? And don't go snooping around where you know you shouldn't. Agreed?"

"I'll do my best." It was not the answer he was looking for, but he accepted it. We held hands a moment longer and then he returned to the lodge.

I walked to the center of town where the main courtyard was. Along the way, I passed three hawks. They were circling me closer than usual. Could it be that Ander had sent them to watch over me? Or were they on patrol for Sebastian? In either case, it seemed unlikely that the birds could communicate much with either party, so they didn't alarm me a great deal. Silas awaited my arrival as promised and wasted no time getting straight to the point.

"Alexa, thank you for coming," he said. He was nervous, edgy, unsure of how to approach the subject he was trying to delve into. "Here's the thing, Alexa—I've been working for your father for some time now. I admire the man, Ganesh and Nicolas too—I think they will do great things for us all. The thing is Alexa, I don't want to get you into any trouble with your father, but I feel I have an obligation to him," he was really nervous, looking down and around in circles, hardly catching my eye.

"What is it, Silas?" I said.

He looked up at me with his deep brown eyes, a frown on

his face, clearly having trouble forming the words he needed to. "I saw your mother yesterday morning when I was delivering mail in Lathbury, and I picked up a letter for you. I knew how much you wanted to hear from her, so I was excited to find you as soon as I could. I looked everywhere. I even asked Grayson, but he just shrugged me off and said you were probably spying around the lodge somewhere. I called your name all over the lodge and walked down every street in town, but I could not find you. I was planning to tell your father I thought you were missing when he returned, but I checked your room this morning and there you were, sound asleep." He paused, advanced to a bench, and sat down. "Naturally, I'm wondering where you were."

Silas was a kind person, and I liked him very much. He was what you might call simple, but not stupid simple. He liked easy answers to life's complications, his lifestyle was exceedingly basic, and he was unaccustomed to confrontation in any form. These things were clear from my brief encounters with him, and I thought humor was my best chance to give him an answer he could live with.

"I travel alone in secret, for I am Alexa, the spy of Bridewell!" I proclaimed in my best comic voice, but he didn't laugh. Instead, he glared at me, and I began to feel uneasy about his motives. I tried my next tactic. "It might be hard to understand, but Grayson and I have an unwritten rule when my father travels and I'm stuck in Bridewell. He pretends to watch over me, and I play spy as much as I want. It's a game, you see? I thought Grayson sent you to flush me out. He's used that trick before, but obviously not this time. Sorry to have worried you."

Silas looked relieved. "Next time I call for you, and you hear me, do me a favor and assume I'm not playing a game."

"It's a deal. And I really am sorry," I said. I hated lying to everyone, and I think the extra apology was more for me than Silas. I knew the day was coming when all my lies would be revealed, and each time I told one I felt significantly worse.

We talked a spell longer and then Silas got up and started to leave. "Oh, I almost forgot," he said, reaching into his breast pocket. "Here's that letter from your mother." He handed it to me and walked off, the lightness of his step clearly showing the weight of the world lifted off his shoulders.

I sat thinking a moment longer, twirling the unopened letter with my fingers, and wondering if Pervis would be sobered up by now.

THE CHESS
MATCH

The emotional distraction I expected my mother's letter to create forced me to shove it into my back pocket unread. I started off in the direction of Renny Lodge, intent on visiting Pervis, but completely unsure of how such a meeting would go. I stopped in one of the classrooms and grabbed a wooden chessboard and a leather bag of matching pieces.

The holding cells were in an area of Renny Lodge that was dark and uninviting. There was one advantage though, which I found refreshing just now—it was below ground, in the basement, and thus cool. Even as dusk approached in Bridewell, the soggy air below ground was a welcome change from the dusty, dry air above. It reminded me of how it felt to be in the tunnels, which in turn reminded me of Yipes, Darius, and the rest. I found myself missing them.

Turning the corner at the last step, I held back and reviewed the scene. Two guards were present, one at the door into the cellblock, the other at a desk, busy with reports of one kind or another. I recognized the man at the desk, but not the other.

"Hello, Mr. Martin. It's been a while since you've had any business down here. How's our guest doing?" I said.

"Alexa, what are you doing here? This is no place for you to be roaming around. You should go exploring somewhere else, especially given the cargo this place is holding," said Mr. Martin.

The man at the door stood motionless and said nothing.

"Has he sobered up yet?" I asked. The man guarding the door smirked and let out a small laugh.

"Let's just say he's been spending a lot of time with his face in a bucket," said the guard.

"Can I see him? He enjoys playing chess, and I thought a game might take his mind off his troubles."

"Now why would you want to make Mr. Kotcher feel better? Everyone knows you two hate each other," said Mr. Martin.

"I know he's a brute, I just—"

"Hold it right there," Mr. Martin interrupted. He was offended, out of his chair and leaning against his desk with both hands in front of him. "We work for him, so as you can imagine we've got mixed feelings about the current state of affairs. A lot of people think he's difficult to deal with, and he surely can be. But he's got his good points too, not the least of which is an everlasting love for Bridewell and all it stands for. If we lose him we lose a measure of security, especially if he stirs up trouble in Ainsworth. Just you remember that when your father runs him out of town."

"I'm sorry, Mr. Martin. I'll try to choose my words more carefully in the future."

"You sound more like a politician every day," said Mr. Martin.

"So, can I go in and see him? I promise not to do anything stupid," I said.

Mr. Martin rolled his eyes. "Oh *all right*. But behave yourself—if you only desire to cause him more misery, I won't hesitate to report you to your father."

"Yes sir."

"Step aside, Raymond; let her through," said Mr. Martin.

The guard opened the door and cool air escaped out into the hallway. It had the subtle sweet smell of vomit hanging over it, just enough to make me gag for a brief moment. Upon entering the cellblock the guard slammed the door shut behind me.

The cellblock contained four rooms with rows of bars, two rooms on each side. There were hard dirt floors, bunks, and nothing on the cold stone walls. The two cells in the rear had small windows high up on the farthest wall back, which let in a faint mist of light. The windows were only about a foot in diameter and had bars running across them.

I heard soft moaning from one of the back cells. A three-legged stool sat next to the doorway and I picked it up. With some difficulty I held the stool, the chessboard, and the bag of chess pieces, and I made my way slowly to the back of the cellblock. Three of the cells were empty; the fourth, on my right in the back, held Pervis Kotcher. He looked dreadful.

At first he did not see me. He was rocking back and forth; sitting on the edge of a cot facing the back wall, staring down into a bucket that was surely full of something unspeakably gross. I dropped the three-legged stool with a bang and began setting up the chessboard a few inches away from the bars to the cell.

The sound of the stool hitting the stone floor had an interesting effect. Pervis attempted to quickly turn around with an impaired wrenching of his neck. It was clear that the sudden jerk of his head caused by the noise sent unearthly pain shooting through his skull. In the next moment, he was on the floor holding his head, writhing in pain, and muttering something about 'that dim-witted girl.' Then, as quick as a rabbit, he was back on his knees, holding the bucket, making a sickening, echoey noise. The quick rise from floor to knees had clearly given him a jolting head rush, and no sooner was he finished with his work at the bucket than he was flat on his back again, moaning quietly.

"Hi, Pervis, how are you doing?" I said, not meaning to be sarcastic, but realizing it sounded that way as soon as I'd said it.

He continued moaning for a few seconds more, then turned toward me and rolled his eyes open. "Whatever it is that you want, please, come back for it later. I've no patience for dealing with you today."

"Actually, I thought you might like some company. I brought a chessboard. Want to play?" I said this with my most exuberant voice, undoubtedly irritating Pervis even more.

Pervis opened his mouth and started to curse at me, and then he seemed to think twice about the idea. He closed his eyes, slowly rose on one elbow, and winced in pain. With his right hand he grabbed the bucket and slid it along the floor with a screech, producing an awful slushy sound from the contents. He spat into the bucket, and then began the slow process of dragging his body off the bed and along the floor. First the arm forward pushing the bucket, and then pulling the rest of his body behind him. Inch by grinding inch Pervis made his way over to the bars while I set up the game. When he finally arrived, he slowly moved to a seated position, hurled a mighty discharge into the bucket, and proclaimed calmly, "What shall we wager?"

Sitting on the stool, I had a bird's eye view of the contents of the bucket, so I retreated to the clammy dirt floor and crossed my legs. For a twelve-year old I was a marvelous chess player. It was a game that came naturally to me. Pervis would not be the first adult I'd made haste of with little or no effort.

"Funny you should ask, I was just wondering the same thing," I said. "If I win, I get to ask you five questions that you must answer honestly, on your honor. If you win, I'll do the same for you."

With some effort, Pervis replied, "What could you possibly know that I would care about?"

I stared at him long and hard.

"A lot," I said.

At some level he seemed to believe me, and a typical Pervis Kotcher smirk crept onto his face. He was looking a measure better, though it might have just been an act to rattle me.

"All right then, you've got yourself a game. On your honor, five questions, answered honestly," he said.

"Deal."

There wasn't much about Pervis I trusted, close to nothing actually. He was a shameless opportunist, a shifty eyed leader to his men, and probably the lousiest drunk I'd ever laid eyes on. But it was known around Bridewell Common that people, even bad people, never wavered from telling the truth once they gave their word. It was this knowledge that made my lying so difficult, even if the lies were intended for good. I believed Pervis would tell me the truth if I got the chance to ask him five questions, because that was just the way of things around these parts. In any case, it was a risk I was willing to take.

"White first. That would be you," I said.

Pervis moved his pawn to g4, a typically meaningless first move for an amateur. This was going to be easier than I thought.

I moved my pawn to b6, playing a waiting game to sniff out his next move. Now the board looked like this, with me at black and Pervis at white:

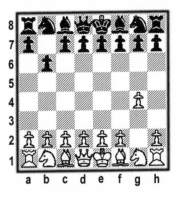

One of my useful tactics was to distract my opponent with offhand remarks or questions.

"I've never seen you drunk before. Why the sudden downward spiral?"

"Sorry, no honest answers, and no talking, until you beat me," said Pervis. Okay, so he was focused, unwilling to partake of my little distractions. Fine, I'll just finish him off faster that way.

The next three moves put me in a good position to start taking pieces with my bishop and my kingside knight, and I was beginning to understand his tactics, however juvenile they might be. Now the board looked like this:

From the looks of it, Pervis had no plan of attack. He was simply countering my moves while he waited for me to reveal a power piece (something I never did early). Unfortunately for Pervis, this strategy was leaving his king wide open for attack with no protection from the center. Yes, this was definitely starting to shape up nicely. At this point in the game we had each moved five times. I gave myself a personal challenge to finish him off in fewer than twenty moves.

Pervis took my pawn at d5. I countered by taking his pawn with mine at d5, followed by Pervis taking my pawn at d5 with his knight from c3. Two moves later, Pervis moved his queen to e2, directly in front of his king. That was odd. He was trying to create a situation where my king would be pinned down by my own pieces. Slightly flustered, I moved my knight to g7.

Pervis moved his knight to f6, leaving the board looking like this:

"Checkmate," said Pervis, which he followed by hawking a big loogie into the bucket.

"You tricked me. You played dumb and I fell for it." I was in a state of disbelief, and I was angry. He'd beaten me in only nine moves. That hadn't happened since I was seven years old.

""I'll go you double or nothing. Ten questions!" I said.

"No thank you, I'll take what I've won and cash out if you don't mind." He shuffled back to the cot, dragging that disgusting bucket as he went. After a monumental effort, he was laying flat on the cot, head on the dirty old pillow that had probably been a fixture of this cell for as long as Renny Lodge had been standing.

"Good old Grob, works every time against over confidant players," said Pervis, a new air of satisfaction in his voice.

"What's a Grob? Are you telling me you cheated?" I said.

"No, cheating would have been much harder than the Grob," said Pervis. He was back up on one elbow, looking as if he were past the peak of his hangover.

He continued, "The Grob opening begins with an ugly looking pawn to g4. Many players would not dream of making such a revolting first move in a serious game of chess. It wrecks the kingside pawn structure with an unprotected advanced flank. But, as you have seen, it offers many tactical shots along unusual opening lines. I began playing the Grob as an opportunity to exercise my tactical skills, but found that a lot of my stronger opponents in Ainsworth would fall for it over and over again."

I had badly misjudged Pervis in regard to his chess playing skills.

"The Grob," he continued, "is an excellent surprise weapon against good players who know and expect all the common openings. I played a Grob blitz against one A-class player at the Ainsworth Chess Club. I won the game in a few moves. Appalled, he demanded that I play the ugly opening again. I did, and I won again. This cycle continued for five games. The Grob won each game to the horror of my stunned opponent." Pervis struggled into a sitting position, obviously healed by the sheer enjoyment of beating me so badly. Strangely enough, I had a new respect for him. He was clearly intelligent, and very good at a game that takes cunning and skill to be great at.

"Let's see, first question needs to be a real eye opener, something to set the tone, don't you think?" he said. He rubbed the weak stubble on his nearly non-existent chin, spat into the bucket, which was now sitting between his legs on the floor, and looked up at me with a big grin on his face.

"Ever kissed a boy before?"

I looked at him with total disrespect.

"I'm twelve years old, Pervis. *Of course* I've kissed a boy before." I said this with an air of indignation, but in reality the only boy I'd ever kissed was my father, and even that was not a common occurrence. We fancied hugs.

"Like I said before," said Pervis, a little flushed, "I can't imagine you knowing anything I don't already know that I'd want to know."

He ran his hands through his unwashed hair and rubbed the back of his neck. Then he looked up at me.

"All right, I've got one," he said. I braced myself for whatever sick idea he could come up with. I imagined he might ask me if I'd ever eaten my boogers, sucked on my big toe, or sniffed my armpits, all of which I had done.

"That night when Warvold died, you were out there a long time. On your honor now, you tell me what happened out there for real," said Pervis.

I thought seriously about lying, but something stopped me. I don't suppose it was any honorable streak I could claim. Something else altogether prompted me to tell the truth. Maybe it was the first signs of desperation from everything swirling out of control around me.

"He died. He was dead a while before I noticed. I was upset about sitting in the dark with his lifeless body, but I pulled myself together. Not long after I figured out he was dead I ran back to Renny Lodge, but not before I opened his amulet and took the silver key that was inside," I said.

"I knew it! I knew you were lying about that night!"

"I never lied, I just omitted certain facts. I'm only telling you this because I need your help, because for some reason I either trust you or I think you're too dense to be the person I'm looking for," I countered.

"What are you talking about—'person you're looking for'—what's that suppose to mean?"

"Is that one of your questions?" I said.

Pervis bit his lip and took a moment to answer. "Yes, it's one of my questions," he finally said.

"In that case, I'm looking for a man named Sebastian," I said.

"Who's Sebastian?" said Pervis, clearly confused beyond all hope. He was either a gifted actor even with a hangover, or he was quickly becoming someone I might be able to trust based on his apparent lack of knowledge.

"How about that one, is that one of your questions?" I said.

"No, no wait, that's not my question."

After a moment of awkward hesitation, he said sheepishly: "Okay, yes, it is my question."

"Sebastian is, as far as I can tell, an escaped slave posing as a citizen of Bridewell," I said matter-of-factly.

After a moment of reflection on what I'd said, Pervis asked, "So you think this is a game coming down here and making up stories to torment me, is that it?"

"Would that be your final question?" I said.

"No! And quit doing that!" He was yelling now, having a hard time keeping control of himself. I was glad for the bars, seeing as it was unclear what Pervis might do if he could get a hold of me.

"Everything all right in here?" It was the guard from outside, with his head all the way in the room from where he'd opened the entrance about a foot.

"Everything is fine, sir. Pervis is just upset I beat him at chess. Can I have a few more minutes please?" I said.

"Only a little longer. We've got to move him and clean out that cell," said the guard, closing the door with a sour look on his face.

Pervis was thinking hard, trying to log all the possible questions he could ask, trying to figure out if I was telling the truth or just trying to drive him crazy. I think the hangover hurt his mental processing power quite a bit, because he sat there mumbling and thinking for a long time. After a while he pushed the bucket out of the way with his foot and looked up at me.

"If what you're saying is true, then I want you to listen carefully. You may not like me much, and to be perfectly honest, I have never thought much of you. You're small, clever, and spirited, which is exactly what I was when I was your age." He paused with an irritated look on his face, held his stomach, and let out a ferocious, gurgling belch.

"Do you know what happens to a tiny, energetic child that has no money, no promise, and no important associations?" he continued, wiping his mouth with a forearm. "He gets beaten.

First by a drunken father, then, living on the street, by bigger children. And at some point it's just life itself that starts kicking that child around. Pretty soon he turns bitter, angry, willing to do anything to gain respect. And whom do you think that child, when he grows up, hates more than anyone else? Of course it's the same youngster that he was, only this one's got the money, the powerful parents, all the opportunity in the world. This one gets it handed to her on a plate. That's a lot for a man to overcome."

Pervis got up and walked over to the bars, putting both hands on them to hold his weary body up.

"This place is peaceful when you're not around, Alexa. Every summer it gets a little harder, and I get a little angrier. I act more like the child I once was. You bring back a lot of bitter memories for me; maybe that fuels my rage, maybe I'm simply unwilling to see anything good in you. The fact is, I haven't had a holiday in twenty years, and it has been longer still since I've been drunk. The thought of coming back here to face another three weeks with you in Bridewell was more than I could take." He slipped down, and for a terrible moment I thought he would crash to the ground unconscious. He caught himself halfway to the floor and struggled back up, leaning heavily on the bars for support.

He continued, evidently about to pass out. "If what you say is true, then understand this, Alexa: I can protect this place better than anyone. I've put my whole life into it, and I'm telling you, I'm your man. So if you're interested, and you're telling the truth, here's my last question," and he slumped down onto the floor in an exhausted heap.

"Can you get me out of here?"

"I don't know," I said, and then I told Pervis Kotcher everything.

ON BECOMING A DENTIST

After leaving the cellblock, I went to my room. Night had fallen on Bridewell while I was talking with Pervis and a full moon was on the rise. I pulled my Jocasta out of its leather pouch. It was beating like a tiny emerald heart; the same as the last time I had checked it. I was anxious to speak with the animals. I wondered if it would wear out faster if I didn't talk to them for a while. Were there any animals around here besides those traitorous cats that I could have a conversation with?

"I think you were right to trust Pervis." It was a voice from the window.

"Murphy!" I yelled.

"Yes, ma'am, back with news from the forest," he said, flipping down off the sill, across the floor, and onto my lap like a hairball on a windy day.

"How did you know about Pervis?" I said.

"I was there the whole time, watching through the little window. You deserve an award for staying down there as long as you did. The smell coming up from that place made me run gagging for fresh air more than once."

"You're a regular guardian angel aren't you, Murphy?"

"Actually, that would be Yipes. He's the one who keeps sending me to watch out for you. He remains concerned for your safety."

"How is he?"

"Doing fine, and he's a lot closer than you might think, hanging in the shadows near the wall. We have a chain of communication that starts with me, goes through Yipes, then Darius, Malcolm, some of the others in the forest that you met, and finally to Ander and the council. Then the messages come back up the line to Yipes, me, and now you." Murphy's tail was twitching back and forth. He darted off to the door with a listening ear, then back to the windowsill, and finally over to the bathroom that separated my father's room from mine. Within a few seconds he was back on my lap.

"I have word from Ander," he said. "He was surprised about Sam and Pepper, but as they are domesticated, he understood how it could happen. After all, they depend on humans for food and water. As to the hawks, Ander thinks the one you saw might be an isolated case, and that the rest of the hawks are still with us. He asked if you knew of anyone in Bridewell who might keep such an animal as a pet."

I thought about everyone I knew who might keep a hawk in Bridewell. But I could think of no one. Other than Yipes, I had never known of anyone keeping a hawk as a pet, let alone anyone around these parts.

"I'm sorry, Murphy, I don't know of anyone with a pet like that. Did Ander say anything else?" I said.

"Only one thing: 'we're running out of time, so get on with it.' Those are his words, not mine. I for one think you're doing a splendid job," said Murphy. "Though I will admit, it does seem to be going a bit slow, don't you think?"

"I have an idea that might help get things moving along, but I'll need your help," I said.

"Absolutely! Pleased to help anyway I can."

I spent the next few minutes filling him in on the details of my plan, and then we started for the library. The first order of business would be getting inside the locked doors. A few years back, a small cat door was added on the wall just left of the double door entryway. No human could fit through the opening with its hinged wood flap, but Murphy would have no trouble navigating what for him would be a wide birth.

It was only around ten o'clock, so people were still milling around Renny Lodge. The smoking room had its usual collection of late night attendants, and I could hear the cooks cleaning the kitchen and preparing things for the next morning. Murphy slinked along side of me down the stairs, looking every which way, his slight feet making a quiet mist of noise like small pebbles dropped onto sand. An occasional creak on a step from my comparatively ample weight was the only noticeable sound the two of us made until we reached the double doors.

I whispered, "There's the cat door. Remember, no noise. Turn the latch on the door slowly or it will make a loud pop when it comes open."

Murphy said nothing as he sized up the trap door. With his diminutive front foot, he pushed the wood flap slightly, then let it swing back. No rubbing on the edges, no squeaky hinges, it swung free and silent. He placed his head against the flap and made his way through the space, letting the flap down slowly from the other side with his long tail. I hardly noticed a sound as he leapt to the knob, balanced on his hind legs, and slowly turned the latch. It made an audible click as it came unlocked, like the sound of a peanut shell cracking open between a thumb and knuckle.

I had told Murphy not to jump down off the knob because I thought the sound of his thud on the floor might wake the cats. He would be waiting patiently, balanced on the other side of the door. I turned the knob slowly, and I could hear the tiny mechanisms inside quietly move around. I could not see Murphy, but I imagined he looked a lot like a circus clown rolling around on a big round ball, quick feet doing small hops as the knob turned and turned under him.

Finally, the door swung free and I reached my hand around

and grabbed Murphy by his surprisingly bony midsection. He was thinner than I had thought under all that fir, certainly no match for either Sam or Pepper, let alone both of them at one time. I set him down on the floor and carefully closed the door behind me.

The library was on the second level, and it had wood flooring. Creaking as I walked was likely to be a problem, so it was up to Murphy to do the hunting. He was light enough not to make a sound while he padded about the aisles to find what we had come for. It would be my job to patiently sit and wait while Murphy found Pepper, hopefully sleeping, and cut off the medallion around his neck. This would be no small feat. The medallion dangled from a thick leather collar attached by a solid gold ring. His only chance would be to cut the leather collar and slide the ring off, then run for the cat door with the ring and the medallion between his teeth, two screeching and clawing cats chasing him all the way. It would have to be a quick operation—*cut, grab, run*—that was the only way.

I signaled Murphy and he nodded and started away from me in the direction of Grayson's office. It was darker in the library than I had expected, and I lost Murphy in the shadows almost immediately. Seconds turned into minutes as I waited. Finally, Murphy returned with news.

I lifted him to my ear. "I found them both curled together in the chair," he whispered. "No sign of any hawks outside the window. With the light it's hard to tell which is which. I know Pepper is darker, but other than that, they're a close match."

"I don't know of any other markings," I whispered back. "If you're not sure, just take the one you can cut off the easiest and get out fast."

I set Murphy down and reached into my pocket to find the weapon I'd fashioned for him. It was a small block of wood. With some effort, I had snapped off the smallest blade on my pocketknife, carved out a slit in the block, and jammed the butt of the small blade into the wood. I took the makeshift leather cutter and placed the wood block into Murphy's mouth. He bit down hard, and I ran my shirt against the sharp edge of the blade as he pushed his head up. It ripped cleanly through.

"If you don't have a clear shot at the medallion, keep the blade in your mouth. It will be your only defense against them," I whispered, then Murphy turned and he was gone, swallowed by the black night of the library. I was immediately sorry I had sent him.

Minutes passed. I heard voices in the distance, the echo of laughter, a clang of a pot or a pan being placed in a sink. Water running. And then I heard an unearthly screech from one of the cats, a sound I could not translate into words. I was terrified for Murphy and I thought my capacity to understand animals had already begun to fade. Without thought I grabbed for the leather pouch around my neck with the stone inside and clutched it tightly.

And then the voices returned. "Stop him! He has the medallion! Kill him!"

It was time for me to move. I opened the door and returned to the hallway. I closed the door firmly behind me, and lifted the flap to the cat door in my direction. All the while I heard a mix of screeching and words and claws on wood. I got down on all fours and placed my head on the floor so I could look through the small opening. There was still no sign of Murphy in the dark.

The sounds were much closer now: "Mrrrrooooeeew!! Don't let it get away!"

A moment later I had to move out of the way as a blast of sliding fur came shooting through the door. It was Murphy, gold ring between his teeth, the medallion dangling below. As soon as he was through, I dropped the swinging door and sat down right in front of it. Murphy tried to stop but continued to slide on the waxed floor. He hit the wall opposite the library with a thud; the gold ring released from his teeth and flew into the air, landing with a loud clang between the two of us. Pepper, the lead cat in the chase, came crashing into the door behind me. Sam landed on top of him and screamed from inside the library. "Get away from the door! Who are you? Return the medallion!" and other more nasty remarks came billowing through the air.

Murphy came to as loud footsteps started from the staircase below.

"Oh, no," I whispered.

"Murphy! Get up, Murphy!" Holding the flap down with one hand I took my knife out of my pocket with the other and opened the largest blade with my teeth. The cats were clawing and pushing against the flap, screeching all the while. I pushed the flap as hard as I could and sent them flipping backwards into the air. With one hard thrust, I slammed my knife into the jam of the little opening. The flap swung down and stopped hard against the blade, locking the cats in for the night.

The approaching footsteps were almost right on top of us. I darted across the floor, grabbed the medallion, and whisked Murphy into my arms, then I tossed Murphy up the stairs to the landing where he hit with a thud. I turned and faced the approaching footsteps coming around the corner.

A man with a wicked looking pair of pliers burst into view and frantically looked up and down the hallway. I had the feeling that he was looking for help, had seen me, and hoped he might do better if he kept looking back and forth a while longer. Sizing me up with a pitiful 'is this the best I can do?' look on his face, he grabbed me by the arm and lurched me off my feet and down the stairs. We entered a first floor classroom and he slammed the door behind us.

The room was used for apprenticing dentists, which I thought was a fascinating line of work. The frantic man, who I now took to be a practicing dentist and teacher using the classroom to make some extra money in the wee hours of the night, dragged me over and stood me in front of another man, strapped down from every which way (including his forehead) to the dentist's chair.

"He's got a prodigious ripper!" said the dentist. "A molar so rotten he couldn't eat a bowl of wind without passing out from the pain."

The patient was squirming as much as he could in an effort to get free, but the straps would have none of it. If there was one thing this dentist could do it was lock a man down and good.

"When I pry open his mouth and remove the cotton, I'll stick a jammer in there to keep it gaping," said the dentist. "Then I'll spin around to hold him steady, and you use these pliers to yank that scurvy monster out!" He continued cursing a blue streak while frantically waving his arms all over the place; then he swaggered into position in front of the patient.

"How will I know which tooth is the right one?" I said.

He looked at me hard. "Little girl, I guarantee you the offensive tooth in question will be abundantly clear when you look inside this man's head," said the dentist.

"Ready... here we go!" he yelled.

The dentist used metal tongs to remove the cotton from the patient's mouth. What came out was such a string of profanity I thought I might have to wash my own mouth out with soap. The patient made the error that the dentist had clearly calculated he would, yelling obscenities with his mouth wide open. In one complete blur of motion, the dentist forced the wood jammer into the man's mouth between the row of teeth opposite where the bad tooth was, spun around behind him, and finished by placing him in a headlock from behind. It was one of the most beautiful things I've ever seen, and still is to this day.

"Stop your gawking and yank that stink bomb!" yelled the dentist. I jumped up on the patient's lap and readied my pliers. He was breathing hard, right into my face, and it smelled horrible—worse than any dead skunk I'd ever passed, worse than any latrine I'd ever been in. This man's mouth *was* a latrine. I thought I might pass out or vomit or both, but I found my composure, held my breath, and moved in.

The dentist was right. The tooth was a solid shade of dark brown, like the leather on my father's saddle, and it had stinky white and yellow stuff oozing out all over. I inserted the pliers just as the dentist was losing his grip on the patient's head.

"Sheep farts!" screamed the dentist, but he managed to re-grip and hold him steady.

I headed back in, and this time, I got a hold of the rotten tooth. I gripped it tight and pulled with all my might. Something came lose and I went flying head over heals off of the patient and somersaulted onto the floor. Dazed, I sat up and tried to get everything back into focus.

"He's choking, get back up here and finish the job!" said the dentist. The patient was definitely gagging on something; this much was clear from the shade of purple his face was turning.

I jumped back up onto his chest and saw that the tooth had come out, but I'd lost it in the fall and it had since tumbled down his tongue and lodged in his throat. I reached down into his mouth, past the slimy ooze where the tooth had been, and pinched the decayed bicuspid between my thumb and forefinger. I immediately flung it out of my hand over my back and wiped my now slobbery hand all over the patient's shirt. I was officially over any desire I might have had to be a dentist.

"Let that be a lesson to you," the dentist said, as he loosened his grip around the man's neck. "Brush your teeth!" And with that, he waved me out of the room and returned to comfort the bawling man with a bill for his services.

I stood dazed in the hallway for a moment, shaking my head and replaying the scene in my mind, then I ran back upstairs as fast as I could, where I found the cats were already meowing with less frequency, the fight almost worn out of them. I quickly advanced up the first set of stairs to find Murphy and get back to my room. To my horror, he remained unconscious, breathing uneasily, blood oozing slowly from a wicked scratch across the front of his head. I carefully picked him up and went to my room, cursing myself for sending him into the library with those awful cats.

My Mother's Letter

I went to the bathroom and got a wet washrag. Murphy was lying still on my bed, shivering and twitching as if dreams of fighting off maniacal cats were racing through his head. I dabbed his wound and cleaned the fur matted with blood around his eyes and nose. What really bothered me was the considerable bump I found on his forehead. It was either from his crash into the wall after the chase, or heaven forbid, from the impact of being thrown onto the landing.

While Murphy remained quiet I dug into my pocket and removed the medallion and the gold ring. Like the one from Sam's neck, this one had a beautiful pattern etched on its surface. I hoped the Jocasta hidden beneath would grant me some new insight I desperately needed. I lifted the throw rug beneath my bed. Under it was a loose floorboard, which I popped out. In the small space below the floorboard I kept my tools, Warvold's silver key, Warvold's favorite book, my mother's broken spyglass, and the printer's glass with its damaged lens.

I removed the printer's glass and covered the hole again with the board and the carpet. When I came back up to the bed, Murphy was sitting up straight, licking one of his paws.

"You're all right!" I placed my hand on his head and petted him gently.

"Couldn't be better. Most excitement I've had since a coyote chased me up a tree a month ago. Quite a good headache, but otherwise, all in one piece," he said.

I was ecstatic to see him up and about. "What happened? Tell me everything," I said.

"Well, let me think—it was dark, hard to get a read on things at first," he said. "I decided my best chance was to wrap my hind legs around Pepper's neck and sit on his head all in one quick motion, then cut the collar, grab the gold ring, and high tail it for the door." He was up on his hind legs acting dramatic.

"As soon as I jumped on his head he jerked and jangled all over the place. I was flying around the room so fast it was dumb luck I was able to hold on at all. I cut the collar, which sent the ring and the medallion soaring across the floor and down the hall. Unfortunately, I also gave the cat a sharp poke in the neck with the knife, and he jerked his head back so hard it threw me in the air like a rag doll. There was a lot of confusion when I landed, but I was closest to the medallion. I ran across the floor, grabbed the gold ring between my teeth, and bolted for the door with both cats behind me."

"Amazing!" I said. Murphy beamed, the proud aura of mythical battle status hanging all about him. The story needed no embellishment; it was first class legend all on its own, and I had a feeling Murphy would be telling the story to children and grandchildren for years to come.

"You got the right one too, the one from Pepper. He was fighting mad when I locked him in the library," I said.

I took the printers glass and set it against the medallion. What I saw rippled like a kaleidoscope in every direction. The broken glass would make it difficult to read the Jocasta. I pulled back, reviewed the glass, and found the largest unbroken piece. Then I got down on the floor on my knees and I pushed the broken lens out of the metal frame. It fell in bits and pieces onto the floor. I took the largest shard of what was left, about a quarter of the whole lens, and sat back up on the bed.

"Do you think it will work?" asked Murphy.

"I think it will, but it may take a while to see everything," I replied.

As it turned out, it was a simple Jocasta—a diagram of three boxes. Two had a line running through them, the third was unattached. The end of the line formed an arrow, which pointed to the third box. It looked like this:

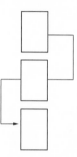

I wrote the diagram down on a piece of paper and cleaned up the glass on the floor. Murphy and I puzzled over the diagram for a few minutes without any idea what it might mean.

Finally, Murphy said, "I'm sorry, Alexa, but I must go report to Yipes. He'll be worried I haven't checked in, and Ander will want an update." He jumped down, ran across the floor, and popped up onto the windowsill. "What do you say I coat our progress with a little honey?" he said.

"Fine by me. Though I'm at a dead end as far as I can tell, and I have no idea what to try next. This Jocasta was my big hope, and it was a flop. Sorry I sent you into all that trouble for no reason," I said.

"Not to worry, I enjoyed it immensely. I'm a wartime hero; they'll probably decorate me with medals and give me a parade when this is all over with. What more could a squirrel ask for?"

He darted out the window and I was alone with my thoughts in the deepest part of the night. It was past one in the morning, and I was utterly exhausted. I reclined on the bed and felt a poke in my back pocket. It was my mother's letter, and now was as good a time as any to get the reading of it over with. With some good fortune I thought it might lull me to sleep.

Alexa,

> *Thank you for your letter. I miss you and your father very much, and even a few lines make me feel closer to you. The daisies are coming up all over town and the garden is full of tomatoes. I told your father not to plant so many, but he wouldn't listen. Now I'm off to the neighbors every three days giving them away, and having them for breakfast, lunch, and dinner. No matter how many tomatoes I eat or give away there are always more the next day. Tell your father I said, 'I told you so'.*

> *I was sorry to hear that you had taken my spyglass to Bridewell. It's hard to discipline you from far away, but you can be sure I'll have you clearing out all the tomato plants from the garden when you get home. I understand the temptation was great, but you really must learn to make better choices. The spyglass was a gift from Renny Warvold. It's the only thing I have to remember her by, so it's special to me. Just bring it home with you and be careful with it. I'll get the lens fixed and you can work off the expense around the house.*

> *How's the weather in Bridewell? I'm sure it's as hot as ever. The River Roland runs even higher than usual this year and keeps Lathbury cool by late afternoon.*

> *Write again! See you and father soon.*

> *Love,*
> *Mother*

The beautiful, ornate spyglass. As soon as I learned it was a gift from Renny I began to understand things in a new light.

Maybe the three boxes on Pepper's medallion were the three sections of the spyglass. The images on the first two could equal whatever was on the third. I scrambled off my bed and ran to the window, looking all around for Murphy, hoping I could catch him. But he was already long gone.

I returned to my hiding spot and removed the rug and the wood panel. My hands shaking, I picked up the broken spyglass and returned to my bed. I extended the sections and revealed all the wonderful paisley patterns that adorned the tubes. Every section was like a vibrant forest of color, and finding the Jocasta's hidden within seemed an impossible task, especially given that I only had a shard of magnifying glass to work with. I began scanning the large, outer tube with the splinter of glass, and quickly realized that it would take hours just to scan the one tube. I was already so tired I could barely keep my eyes open.

I went to the bathroom and listened for my father's steady snoring. It swept into the night, a quaint little snore, not too loud, almost soothing. I took water from the basin and wetted my face and neck, hoping it would revive me. Then I returned to the bed and began scanning again.

It was hopeless. At the rate I was going it would take days to find the hidden Jocastas, and I was already bobbing my head as I tried to stay awake; before long I would collapse from exhaustion and wake up with Sam in my face and Sebastian towering over me with a sledgehammer. I pulled back and rubbed my eyes. There had to be another way. It was past two in the morning and I couldn't stay alert for much longer.

I held the spyglass at arm's length and turned it slowly in my hand, looking for a pattern that might join the three tubes together. I placed one hand under the largest tube and one on top of the smallest tube and continued spinning the whole thing around. The three patterns did seem to have a point at which they matched, but they were not lined up between the three sections. I took the top and bottom tubes in hand and to my surprise, with a fair amount of effort, I was able to slowly twist them in opposite directions. When the patterns lined up, the tubes snapped into place and stopped. It had never occurred to me to turn the tubes in this way before.

Now I could see a line of commonly shaped paisley swirls, one on top of the other, each slightly larger than the last, in a row down the three tubes. The color also ran light to dark from the first pattern to the last. At the center of each paisley pattern was a symbol, which looked like a flash of yellow light. I picked up my shard of glass and moved in tight to view the center of the pattern on the first tube. I had found the first of three Jocastas.

It was an image of a man, eyes missing, groping his arm up and out against an invisible object. I immediately recalled the fable Warvold shared with me on the night of his death about the blind men and the elephant, and I understood the invisible object to be the elephant in Warvold's story.

My heart was racing and I was all at once wide-awake as I moved to the next tube. The Jocasta on this tube depicted a man on his knees, arms raised in worship to an unseen god.

I moved to the last tube, and found an even simpler Jocasta than the one on Sam's medallion. It was nothing more than a capitol letter 'S'.

Elephant + Worship = Sebastian.

I was more confused than ever.

THE MEETING ROOM

Extreme fatigue is an overpowering force. Under the right circumstances it blankets its captive under heavy layers of deep sleep, layers that must be peeled away to reach beneath. As voices and light from the wakeful world pound to get in, they fight against a thick film to wrench the weary back to life.

"Wake up, Alexa, wake up!" How long had I been out? How long had a squirrel been screaming at me in his squeaky voice? This is all a dream, all of it; the talking animals, the wall, and the rodent doing cartwheels on my chest—all a delightful dream.

The squirrel had his face in mine now, his mouth wide open, revealing a surprisingly stout set of teeth. He bit down softly, then harder, right over my nose, and I was awake.

"Murphy!" I yelled as I jerked up into a sitting position, sending him head over heels off the end of the bed with a harsh thud. The first soft light of morning crept over the wall into the room. My clock read 5:43 a.m.; I had slept for almost four hours.

Murphy climbed onto the bed looking dazed. "You're getting into a bad habit of tossing me around rooms."

"All in a day's work for a hero," I countered, and then added a profound apology.

"There's trouble, Alexa. The slaves are on the move. Ander thinks the invasion will begin tomorrow night."

152

"Then we must hurry." I spent the next few minutes telling Murphy what I had discovered during his absence. Once wound up, it takes a great deal of effort to get him calmed down again, and news of my progress sent Murphy into a fit of enthusiasm. I finally had to grab him by the midsection and hold him in midair to calm him down. After a few seconds, he hung there, limbs dangling, chest heaving up and down.

"Let's not get too excited. We still don't know Sebastian's real identity, and I fear we've run out of time. I think what we've discovered can still do some good, but I'll need your help to make sure," I said.

I knew he would be willing to go on another errand, and I quickly explained what I needed him to do and sent him on his way. He would be gone for more than an hour. As for me, the sun was coming up and the time had come to talk with my father.

I crept into the bathroom, quietly opened the door to his room, and peeked inside. His room was dark except for the ray of light pouring in from where I stood. The light turned everything a glowing shade of shallow orange. His familiar deep breathing filled the space. I tiptoed to the other side of the bed and crawled under the covers. It was warm, and I had to overcome the urge to sleep again.

"Father?" I whispered, then again, only louder: "*Father?*"

He stirred and rolled to his side facing me, smacking his lips and rubbing his eyes. His hair was formed into a high golden arch, which made me laugh out loud. My father opened his eyes.

"Alexa. How nice to see you," he said in a dreamy voice, and then his eyes slowly shut once more. I called his name again and this time he sat up, fully awake.

"Is everything all right?" he asked.

"I'm tired, but yes, I'm fine." We looked at each other for a long moment.

"I have a lot to tell you," I said.

"What do you mean?"

I sat up and wrapped the thick blanket from the bed around my shoulders and told my father all the details of the previous few days. Well, almost all the details. Midway through I decided the notion of talking animals was something I would keep a secret. It served no purpose to tell him, and I had grave concerns about how the knowledge might be put to use once word spread in and around Bridewell.

When I was finished, I asked him the question I had been asking myself all morning: "Who do you think Sebastian is?"

He rubbed the stubble on his flushed cheeks and gazed thoughtfully across the room.

"I don't know, but we must share what you've learned with the others," he said. "Get dressed and be in the meeting room in half an hour." He rose from the bed and walked to the bathroom, stretching his arms over his head and lowering them again as he went. I remained motionless, afraid to move, the warm blanket still surrounding me. He splashed water on his face, then turned to me, water dripping from his thick beard. "Get up, Alexa. There's no time to waste." It was an order, not a request.

I crawled out of the big bed and touched my feet on the chilly wooden floor. As I walked past him into my own room I brushed up against his legs and he knelt down beside me. He placed his giant hands on my shoulders, and I realized something new about my father, something I had never thought of before. If he chose to, he could crush me with those monstrous hands; it would take him almost no effort at all. Instead, as if aware of my new understanding, he pulled me close and hugged me for a long time, my small head in his hand, and he whispered in my ear: "What am I to do with you, my crafty little girl?" And then he released me and returned to his work at the washbasin, running both hands through his golden funnel of hair.

With my bathroom door closed I dressed and prepared myself for the meeting. I wore my green long sleeved shirt, a red button up vest, and a brown armless tunic with a brightly colored hem down the front. I topped it off with my snug leather cap and tucked my hair behind my ears. A short while later I heard the door to my father's room open and close, his footsteps pounding in the hall and down the stairs until I could discern his movements no more. I opened my window and looked all around for Murphy, but an hour into his task he was nowhere to be found.

I picked up my bag and trudged down the hall in the direction of a mysterious room I had never stepped foot in.

One day last summer I was so bored that I began sneaking around Renny Lodge hiding under tables and behind couches near the walls. It was a fun diversion on an otherwise dull afternoon, and I found myself enjoying the thrill of pretending to be a spy. I had turned every person in the Lodge into an evil character in my plot to find some make believe hidden treasure I can't recall. Lost in my own world, I found myself concealed behind a thick purple curtain near the meeting room. To my surprise, the door to this mystifying room opened and Ganesh appeared, followed by Warvold, and then my father. I pulled the curtain back a little more and peeked inside as the door began to shut, but I only saw a sheet of light streaming in from an enormous window, glaring against silhouettes of objects in the room. As the door creaked shut, a large hand touched my shoulder, locked down, and pulled me from behind the curtain.

"I've told you not to sneak around. It's for your own good, so please obey me." It was my father. The way he had said it wasn't mean, but it was forceful and stern. He wandered off towards the kitchen then and left me with my heart racing. I have never since gone near that room.

And here I was, being invited into that very place only a year later, a shiver trembling through my body as I stood at the closed door. I looked to my left and saw the heavy velvet curtain hanging in a bunch against the wall. Then I grabbed the handle, opened the door, and went inside.

The meeting room was brisk and humorless with dark tile flooring and shadowy walls with nothing on them. Inkwells and worn old pens adorned two long, facing tables in the middle of the room. Stark terracotta water pitchers and cups were placed on the tables along the edges. It was a plain room, a business room, a room without character or charm. I closed the door behind me, leaving only natural light from the imposing window on one side. Morning dust was in the air, golden and swirling in the sunlight, dancing about as people became quiet and moved into their seats behind the tables.

Everyone was present: Silas, Ganesh, Nicolas, my father, Grayson, and even Pervis, chained to a chair, hands in shackles, dutifully overseen from behind by a club wielding guard.

We moved to our seats, my father with Ganesh on his left and me on his right. Nicholas sat next to me, and across from us at the opposite table were Silas, Grayson, and the shackled Pervis.

The last thing I remember hearing before my father began was the unfortunate sound of Pervis shifting in his wooden chair and moving the chains around his ankles. This produced a chilling clang that echoed off the high ceiling, reminding us all of his grim circumstance.

"Thank you for coming to such an early meeting," my father began. "It means a great deal to me that you would accommodate my desire to talk with you. Assuming Pervis is adequately secured, I must now ask the guard to leave us to our privacy." The guard checked over Pervis to be sure of his handiwork, then made his way toward the door.

"Guard," said my father, "leave me the keys." The guard returned and stood before my father, unhitched the keys from his belt, and placed them on the desk. Then he turned and left the room.

The chamber sufficiently sealed, my father continued.

"As you all know, losing Warvold has been a serious blow to Bridewell. Ainsworth senses our new weakness, and they may take advantage of us. More and more people are trying to settle here, and we have nowhere to put them. Our head guard is in shackles, leaving us vulnerable to attack and his men without a leader. And there are other, more sinister plots afoot that we may not even be fully aware of.

"Grayson has been here longer than anyone; he is an old and dear friend. Silas is a new addition to this group, but someone I feel we can trust. Nicholas is new as well, but clearly a gifted leader, and someone who will no doubt be an important part of our future. My dear friend Ganesh—words cannot express how important you are to Bridewell and what will become of it. I have also invited Alexa to join us this morning. The need for her presence here will become clear in a moment."

He paused and looked at our chained companion. "And Pervis. What will become of you? I fear we have made a mistake in locking you up, but I can't bring myself to set you free."

As my father poured a glass of water from a pitcher on the table I became aware of a strange movement from the edge of the large facing window. It was small, almost unnoticeable, like a twig caught in a spider's web, dangling on a puff of air. Murphy was back.

His body was hanging outside the sill by one paw, and he was waving with his other paw to get my attention. He kept waving and waving. Then the little leg shot out of site and I heard a faint 'flit' as he lost his grip and scraped along the outer wall.

"Father, might I stand at the window for some fresh air? The dust is a bit thick," I said. He nodded yes and continued talking.

"A week ago Alexa discovered a way outside the wall, and she just completed two days in the mountains and the forest before returning here yesterday."

A collective gasp filled the room. "Have you lost your mind? She could have been killed out there!" said Ganesh.

Grayson looked as though he would rather have been under the table where no one could see him, and poor Silas stared at me as if my lies had broken his heart.

While the group asked questions of my father, I arrived at the window, placed my back against the wall, and felt blindly along the edge for a furry mass. Murphy was gone, but he had left me a gift on the flat of the stone sill. I picked it up.

"Listen to me," my father said with a raised voice, and the room grew quiet again. "Alexa did this on her own accord without my knowledge or permission. But I think we will all be thanking her before this meeting is over." My father shot an accusing look at Grayson who sat slack-jawed and gazing across the room.

"While Alexa was outside the wall she discovered a narrow tunnel that led to a position from which she could see an underground chamber," said my father. "The chamber is part of a labyrinth of underground tunnels created from the mining effort to build our walls. The tunnels and chambers wind all around The Dark Hills and even directly under Bridewell itself. A group of people, people with 'S's branded on their foreheads and high on their cheeks, live within these tunnels."

"Why that's preposterous!" yelled Nicholas. "Do you realize what that would mean?"

Everyone else sat motionless, some with mouths hanging open, calculating the implications of such a fact. I was back in my seat, and my father nodded to me. I removed a wooden tube from my bag and handed it to him.

"I'm afraid it's true," he said. "I have a map here that shows the layout of all the tunnels and chambers. Another collection of tunnels resides above ground covered by thick brush, which is how the slaves maneuver without detection, scrounging for food and water.

"These men are angry, and they have been plotting to enter Bridewell and take it over for years. They could attack the city as early as tomorrow night, and we are inadequately prepared to deal with such an attack."

"This can't be possible," said Ganesh. "We sent those prisoners back. Warvold escorted them all the way to Ainsworth. I tell you this *cannot* be possible!"

"I'm sorry Ganesh, but as much as I wish none of this were true, I don't think Alexa is making these things up. Please, just let me finish. I have more I need to tell you, and then you can ask all the questions you want." Everyone went momentarily quiet and still. The faces across from me expressed shock and confusion.

"Warvold was a mysterious man, and his wife Renny was maybe even a little more baffling than he was. As you know from our conversations with Nicholas, she was fond of a certain kind of artwork called a Jocasta. She was kind enough to leave these veiled treasures hidden all around us, and Alexa has used them to help solve a puzzle I think both Renny and Warvold wanted us to figure out after they were gone. We have to face the fact that Warvold's death set in motion the end of Bridewell as we know it. What that means is still a mystery, but one thing is certain—we're not all on the same side in the battles that will soon be waged."

I pulled a piece of paper from my pack and handed it to my father. "This is a drawing of a Jocasta Alexa found hidden within a medallion on one of the library cat's collars. For those of you who may not know, those cats used to belong to Renny Warvold. As you can see from Alexa's drawing, the image shows three boxes, two connected, that when joined together clearly equal the third." I pulled the spyglass out of my pack, extended the three sections, and handed it to my father.

"The three boxes on the Jocasta represent the three sections of this spyglass, which was given to my wife as a gift from Renny Warvold. Each of the three sections on this spyglass contains another Jocasta, and it is within these that an important message is revealed."

My father pointed his finger to the first tube in the spyglass. "The Jocasta on the first section depicts a man groping at an object above and to his side." Pointing to the second tube, he continued: "The Jocasta on the second section reveals a human figure, kneeling with arms raised, praying to an unseen god. And here, on the third section, the Jocasta is nothing more than a simple letter 'S'."

My father paused and looked around the room at the confused faces staring back at him.

"Fascinating," said Nicholas. "The slaves, the labyrinth of spooky tunnels, the messages all hooked together through my mother's art projects. It's a bit far fetched to say the least. Nonetheless, your daughter spins a mighty good tale, and I can't help but want to hear the outcome."

Without further comment, and the reassurance of a nod from Grayson and Silas, my father went on with what I had shared with him earlier that same morning.

"On the night when Warvold died, he told Alexa a story. It was about six blind men who all felt an elephant and thought it was something different because of the part they were touching. One touched the tail, another the side, yet another the head, and so on. Thus the depiction in the first Jocasta stands for an elephant. The symbol on the second Jocasta is self-explanatory—it represents the worship of some unknown god. The letter 'S' on the final section might have held no meaning to Alexa had it not been for her encounter with the slaves."

It was here that my father motioned me to rise and speak, and I lied to protect the animals. "According to two slaves I watched and listened to in the underground chamber, there is a traitor living among us," I said. "This man is their leader and goes by the code name Sebastian, thus the letter 'S'."

A burst of gasps again filled the room, not the least of which was from Ganesh as he looked at me with horror on his face.

"You've gone too far now, Daley. Stop with this nonsense!" he shouted.

"Really you two, this is too much," said Grayson.

There was a mixture of mumbling around the room, and then a voice was heard that no one expected.

"I personally helped escort the slaves to Ainsworth." It was Pervis, his head down, facing the floor.

He looked up then, and surveyed the room from side to side. "Only thing is, Warvold stayed in Ainsworth for several days after my guards and I returned to Bridewell. It could be that he bought their freedom, or otherwise convinced Ainsworth to set them free outside. He was a peculiar man and he often made secret, unusual decisions with implications only he understood. Don't think for a minute that he didn't expect things to unravel as they have. We may yet see his wisdom in all this before we're through." He scraped his chains across the table, turned, and gestured towards the window.

"In any event, we've known for a long time that things move around in The Dark Hills. My guards and I see it all the time. Maybe now we know what those things are."

"Oh come on Pervis, this is simply ridiculous!" Nicholas exploded. "Are you telling me you believe the fantasies of a child?"

For the first time since I had entered the meeting room I felt conviction and courage and even some anger. So much at stake, and such closed minds. It would take something more concrete to get this group to believe. I pushed my chair out and walked to the window. I stood for a moment with my back to the group and observed the sickening stone wall. It looked almost alive with its green ivy veins shooting in all directions. When I turned around to address the men, I had a new passion in my eyes.

"I have more to tell."

THE DARK HILLS DIVIDE

All my apprehension was gone. The people sitting at the tables, the things I knew were true about the slaves, the meeting room itself—none of it scared me any longer. Years behind the wall had blinded these men to the world outside. But the wall had taken more than their freedom to experience the outer world. I could see that it had stolen their ability to discern the truth.

I unfolded the paper Murphy had left for me on the windowsill.

"When I ventured outside the wall I met a remarkable man. This man has lived in the mountains for many years, and he has extraordinary abilities with animals. He has been watching the slaves, and he gave me this note."

"Did this man give you a name?" asked Grayson. I nodded yes and told him the man's name was Yipes. He questioned me again, this time about the man's size, and I told him he was the smallest man I'd ever seen. Grayson turned a ghostly white and looked at me with a blank stare, then he put his elbows on the table and dropped his head into his hands.

"What is it, Grayson?" said Ganesh. Grayson looked up, scanned the faces in the room, and answered.

"I think she might be telling the truth." Everyone was looking at Grayson now, trying to figure out what he was talking about.

CHAPTER 21

"Yipes is no legend, he's real. He's a very small man; more than likely able to communicate with animals, and he lives in the wild." Grayson continued his stammering and began shaking his head. He stood up and looked around as though he was trying to recall a distant memory and remember it properly before speaking.

"When he was a boy he lived in Bridewell for a time. He arrived from Ainsworth, and wandered the streets until he was hungry enough to steal bread." He stopped and looked directly at me, then continued. "He stole that bread from me, and I caught him. After that, I let him stay in the library and sleep on the chair in the corner. He was so small; nobody ever took notice of him. When people came in, he hid in the shadows. I brought him scraps from the kitchen and read him books." Grayson walked to the window, drawing out the memory, gazing at the ever-present stone and vine of the wall.

"One day I rounded the corner to the chair and found him sitting in Warvold's lap. I was shocked, afraid old Warvold would get rid of both the boy and me. But I could not have been more wrong. Warvold loved the boy. He would sit and read to him and they would talk of things I only heard in whispers, of talking animals, of things in the wild outside the wall, of secret passages and things of the distant past only Warvold understood. I thought it was all rubbish." He turned and faced the room, leaning against the windowsill, his body outlined against the morning light.

"I went about my business, cared for the boy, and taught him what I knew. Warvold was a busy man in those days, and often he would be absent for weeks on end before returning. Yipes was remarkably agile and strong for his size. He would stack books on the top shelves when no one was about. He could scale a tall bookshelf in an instant, hang by one hand, and stack volume after volume perfectly on a shelf.

"I don't know how old he was when he arrived, nor have

I any idea what his age was when he disappeared a year later. I only know that he told me he would find a way outside, and that when he did, he would live in the wild with animals and learn to communicate with them. Warvold told him so, and he believed. He was treated badly by humans, forgotten, discarded. In the wild, he believed things would be different."

Grayson was visibly moved by his own recollections. He seemed overcome by the idea that this boy he once cared for was still alive, living out his days in the mountains and the forest.

"One day I came into the library and Warvold was sitting in the chair sobbing, holding a strange silver key between his fingers. 'He's gone' he said, 'never to return.' I guess Warvold was right, because I have not seen Yipes since."

The room was quiet. I felt it was my best chance to reveal what little else I knew, to convince them that trouble was indeed on the way. So I read the note from Yipes I had sent Murphy to get. And in the reading, I felt a chill in my bones.

The Dark Hills divide cannot protect you from an evil that lurks within. When the sun sets twice more, he will signal them, and they will come for you. Your only hope is to tear down what you have built.

"It's signed by Yipes," I said. After that, there was a look on the faces in the room I had never seen before in all my visits to Bridewell.

Suspicion.

A SECRET PLAN

After I read the note from Yipes the meeting room was quiet for a long time. It was as if nobody knew what to say or do next, or even how to act. My father was the one to finally break the silence.

"It seems we are all having trouble coming to grips with the situation at hand. Unless anyone objects, I suggest we let Alexa tell us everything else she knows. If what she has already explained to us is true, and it appears that it is, then we have almost no time to prepare for a possible invasion." Pervis shifted in his chair and started the chains jingling between his legs. I was glad to have him in our midst.

I rose and advanced to the far end of the room where a large wooden table surrounded by chairs was kept. My father unhitched Pervis and escorted him to a chair at the new table, then locked him to one of the legs. I invited everyone else to join us and sit down, and I unrolled the map onto the middle of the table. I used heavy brass candlestick holders to keep the map flat against the wood.

"We haven't got a lot of time and we lack proper defenses. Many of those who normally reside in Bridewell are gone for the time being, so fewer are at risk. We have the six of us and how many guards do we have, Pervis?"

"We have fourteen, fifteen if you take these shackles off

of me. We could call on Ainsworth to help us, but they may have let the slaves go to begin with, so I'm not sure how much help they would offer," said Pervis.

"Yes, but fourteen guards?" said Silas; obviously assuming we would not be letting Pervis go. "There could be hundreds of slaves out in those hills. There's no way we could handle them all, especially since we don't know how or when exactly they will strike. And worse, one of them is inside the wall. It could be anyone. Even one of us."

Silas had voiced what all of us were thinking but were afraid to say. What if Sebastian was someone in this very room?

"I refuse to believe that," said my father. "The only one of us who hasn't been in this group for years and years is you, and you don't strike me as an evil mastermind. Besides, whoever this Sebastian is, if he is at all, he would have to keep a low profile to last this long in Bridewell. I suggest we not worry so much about the spy and stay focused on the invasion, which is coming whether a spy exists or not."

What my father was saying resonated with the group. "My hunch is we've already locked up Sebastian anyway," added Nicholas, with a weary eye towards Pervis.

The implication bothered me, and Nicholas had caught me at a time when I was ready to stand up for Pervis when no one else was. This was the opportunity I was looking for to try and get him out of has shackles.

"I don't think pointing fingers at Pervis will solve any-thing," I protested. "We have no evidence to suggest that he is Sebastian. In fact, he is probably the last person among us who we should distrust. He's the only one who was working directly with Warvold before the slaves even arrived in Bride-well. Besides, we have a much better chance of success if he is free to lead our few trained guards in a battle plan."

"She's right," said Grayson. "I've been in Bridewell longer than him, but when I started working in the Library, Pervis was already a part of Warvold's inner circle."

Within a few minutes the group agreed that it was exceedingly unrealistic to think Pervis could be Sebastian. It was further agreed that he was indeed worth more to the cause as a free man than one imprisoned. The group agreed on a new charge against him, drunken and disorderly conduct, and he was released with a stern warning to behave himself.

"Glad to have you back," I said, as Pervis rubbed his wrists where the harsh metal of the shackles had worn his skin raw.

"Happy to be back at work. I hate holidays," he replied.

We were ready to review the map and begin forming a plan, and I leaned over the table so I could better see the details in the natural light pouring in from outside.

"If you look at the map, you'll see that the brown colored lines represent the above ground paths," I said. "The black lines represent the ones below ground. A number of black lines run below Bridewell, but only one seems to have any strategic significance. That one there," I placed my finger on a black line out in The Dark Hills and ran my finger along the map, winding my way toward the center until the line ended. "I believe this spot represents the courtyard in the center of town, and that the slaves have continued digging until this tunnel ends a few feet beneath the cobblestones. When the time is right for them to strike, I think they will break through the cobblestone and pour into Bridewell like so many rats out of a sewer."

Nicholas took his turn at leaning over the map and tried to calculate the distance and direction of the line I was pointing to. "I do believe she's right on that one, that does look like the center of town. You see the lodge is here with the adjoining wall along its side. Either Alexa is right, or it's somewhere close to the courtyard." He looked up and smiled at me, and my anger with him over his accusation of Pervis subsided considerably.

"There's more," I continued. "As long as we move quickly and secure the city so that no one is allowed in or out, the slaves have no way of knowing that we've discovered their plan. I believe the spy and the slaves communicate using a hawk to carry messages back and forth. It gets complicated with the animals, but Yipes has a hawk of his own."

I went on to explain that during the past few hours, Yipes' hawk had been flying over The Dark Hills, looking for signs of a place where the slaves might rendezvous with their own hawk to send and receive messages.

"My hope is that by now the hawk the slaves and Sebastian were using to communicate has been apprehended. If Sebastian does try to correspond further with the slaves, his hawk will be difficult to find, since Yipes should have it caged up in the mountains by now. As long as Bridewell is locked down, messages to The Dark Hills should be halted as we plan for the attack."

A look around the room revealed wide eyes and drooping jaws. It was nice for now that they had no knowledge of the army of animals who were responsible for most of the progress I had made.

"Our best chance is to allow the slaves to continue with their plans to attack the city, and to allow for this attack to take place at night. If Yipes is right, and our location guess is correct, the slaves will attack at the center of town tomorrow night."

"But that's not enough time to mount a plan against them, Alexa. We should contact Yipes and see if the attack can be thwarted from the outside," said my father.

"No, I disagree," argued Pervis. "Right now we have the element of surprise working against them. It may be our only chance to catch them off guard. What we need is a plan, and I think I'm onto something that will work." Pervis looked at the map thoughtfully, then asked for the note from Yipes and re-read part of it aloud. "'Your only hope is to tear down what you have built.' I can't get that out of my mind, and I think I know what he meant for us to do."

The next few hours were spent planning our strategy and working out everything that could go wrong. Everyone agreed it was a brilliant plan, but there was a lot of anxiety about whether it could be done in time. It was noon when we finished our planning, leaving us about thirty-six hours until the slave invasion was expected to begin.

A town meeting was held in the main hall of Renny Lodge, and all the men residing in Bridewell were put to work on projects relating to the scheduled assault. We had sixty-five men including the guards. All four of the gates into Bridewell were locked and heavily guarded, and no travelers were allowed in or out. If a spy did live among us, it was essential to our plan that his ability to communicate with the slaves and move about freely was eliminated.

The town was in a fever of activity by the time night arrived. Everyone, including my father and Nicholas, was engaged in the effort. I became so tired after darkness enveloped the town that I fell fast asleep sitting up against a wall. My father carried me to my room and put me into my bed. I awoke, half dreaming, as he got up to leave.

"How are you doing?" I asked in a sleepy voice.

"All things considered, not bad. It's a lot to process so quickly."

"I know what you mean," I said. "How are things coming along with the work?"

"Just fine. It will be close, but I think we'll make it. You get some sleep now."

He approached the door to leave, then turned as if to say something more. Instead he just looked at me, and I saw that his thick auburn hair had swished into the shape of an 'S' against his forehead. He brushed it away with his brawny left hand, and departed down the hall as I drifted off to sleep.

A MYTHICAL CREATURE

"Blast that Pervis! All the strawberry jam is gone. He must have snuck in here and finished it off last night."

It was morning and I was in the kitchen, energized from my first full night of sleep in almost a week. Grayson was in a sour mood, and I was trying my best to cheer him up.

"Tell you what, Grayson, if things go well tonight, I'll get Silas to bring in a cart full of strawberries and you can eat jam all day long if you like."

The smell of fresh baked breads and tangy slices of red and green apples filled the kitchen. While I stacked my plate with both, Grayson picked up a biscuit and contemplated its size and shape.

"My irritation is made complete by the perfection of biscuits just out of the oven. It would be sinful to eat them plain." He tossed the biscuit onto the table with disgust, sending sparks of crumbs flying in every direction.

I ate ravenously and drank milk in great gulps, my body still searching for fuel to fill some unknown reserve. When I looked up again from my plate, Grayson was inspecting something new he had pulled from his pocket.

"I believe this belongs to you, does it not?" said Grayson, holding my pocketknife. "I assume you had a reason for leaving it where it was, so I pushed a bookshelf in front of the cat door before I removed it. The cats seem agitated and they whine and scratch at the door a lot. Any idea why that might be?"

I had completely forgotten about Sam and Pepper. I took a drink from my glass to buy some time and consider a good answer.

"Keeping them locked up for now would be a good idea," I replied, wiping away a milk mustache with the back of my hand. "It's hard to explain, but they could cause us trouble if you release them. Maybe once everything settles down I'll tell you more, but I can't right now." Grayson nodded his approval and jammed a big spoonful of slimy looking oatmeal into his mouth, then he handed me the knife and looked down at his bowl, rolling his spoon around in its soupy contents.

"You know, he had no name," said Grayson.

"Who?"

"Yipes. He had no name when I met him. His parents, whoever they might be, left him in the streets. He told me he lived in the Ainsworth Orphanage for a while, but they never bothered to name him. He was more of a number in that hellish place, and a small number at that."

"It's a very strange name he decided on," I said.

"That it is," said Grayson through a mouthful of food. "But I'm partial to it, since I helped him pick it out."

As Grayson remembered it, the two of them had been stacking books on a frosty winter day in the library when Grayson came upon a very old volume that was broken and cracking at the seams. He took it to his office and began restoring it while Yipes watched from his perch on the desk. When he finished with his mending, Grayson flopped the book open and began turning the pages to inspect the repaired joint. They came upon a particular page and Yipes exclaimed, 'Read that one to me,' for though he was good at putting away books, he could not read them when he arrived in Bridewell.

The book itself was filled with mythical creatures and

beasts, pure fantasy from cover to cover. Some pages included pen drawings of monsters and strange beings from even stranger places. The page that Grayson had landed on included a picture of a bizarre creature: small, and apparently half monkey half man. As Grayson read, it became clear that this thing they had stumbled upon had, oddly enough, many qualities in common with our little friend. The creature was undersized and could climb and jump with amazing agility. It did not trust humans, and remained hidden whenever men were about.

"Those odd, mythical creatures were called 'Yipes' in the book. As soon as I finished reading that section, we both agreed it was the perfect name for him."

Grayson observed his bowl with a blank stare. The story had brought a rush of memories back to him.

"He's doing well, Grayson," I offered. "Life outside is what he told you it would be, only better."

Grayson raised his head and looked at me with deep appreciation. Our conversation had renewed his strength in ways that food could not, and we were both ready to get back to work.

We left the kitchen together and walked through the center of town, which bustled with activity in every direction. The men, a full night without sleep, looked tired and beaten. The work was steady but slow. Even Pervis barely stood, leaning against a wall, as he shouted orders among the men. I approached him cautiously and asked how things were going.

"Not well, Alexa. We underestimated the work this would take. At the rate we're going we'll never finish by dark," he said. "Ganesh and your father talked it over, and they gave me orders an hour ago. I've sent Silas to quietly round up more men in Lathbury, and Nicolas is doing the same in Lunenburg. They think if we get twenty fresh men by midmorning we have a chance." Nobody voiced the obvious concerns about the risks of sending Silas and Nicolas off on their own; we just looked at one another and shrugged, hoping for the best.

Grayson grabbed hold of two shovels and handed one to me. "Time to make some blisters," he said, and the rest of the day was lost in a haze of sweat and dust.

Hours later, when darkness began falling over Bridewell, a heavy wind was whipping through the courtyard, stinging tired eyes and clogging heaving lungs with thick dust. Despite the conditions and fatigue, men who had worked around the clock continued with an inhuman stamina, and fresh workers gathered in secret by Silas and Nicholas helped lighten the load.

"Storms coming," I observed. Grayson rose from his work and stood beside me, leaning hard against the wall as the wind parted his meager head of hair. We saw Pervis coming from the direction of Renny Lodge. He approached us slowly, shirt flapping uncontrollably at his sides, the wind directly in his face in great gusts.

"We'll make it by dark. Just finishing things up now," he yelled through the wind. He looked beaten but alert, alternately watching the guards at the near tower and the work on the ground.

An hour later, with night fully upon Bridewell, we finished the work. No streetlamps were fired; only a blush of soft moonlight remained on the town square. Families hunkered down in their homes as tired men milled around the completed work with anticipation. The kitchen staff prepared kettles of soup and fresh loaves of bread, and the men formed a line outside Renny Lodge. At the door they took a bowl and a spoon, then my father poured the soup and handed each man a small loaf of bread. Inside, tables were set in the smoking room, and a great fire raged in the fireplace.

There was a strange aura that hung over the room as we sat elbow to elbow sipping from our bowls, listening to the wind buffet against the shutters that had been closed over the windows. It was a harrowing sound, as though the slaves were pounding to get in and tear the place apart. A few sips into dinner all the men went back outside clutching lumps of bread, too skittish to sit inside making chitchat over bowls of broth.

Only my father and I remained.

"You've been working hard," said my father.

"I don't mind," I replied.

"I think it's time for you to go, Alexa. I want you sealed up tight in your room, door locked, until this thing is over. No more running around," he said. The thought of what was coming scared me and I was happy to obey his request. We hugged, and then I retreated to my room and locked the door behind me.

THE PAPER STORM

It was 10:35 when I arrived at my open window, door locked behind me, a thick wind tossing my hair. I hadn't been paying any attention, but clouds were rolling in. Storm clouds. Within a few moments, the moon was gone, and the unlit town of Bridewell below was as black as The Dark Hills had ever been. I could not differentiate between the inside and the outside of the wall, and for a brief moment, it seemed as though the wall itself was a myth, and Bridewell was open, sprawling into the hills uncontained. But the clouds continued to move and part of the moon cast its revealing light against the ivy-covered wall. As quick as the wall had disappeared, it was back in all its awful glory.

Almost eleven. I was holding Warvold's favorite old book, *Myths and Legends in the Land of Elyon*, the one I'd gotten from Grayson. After my visit outside the wall its title was newly intriguing. I had never thought of our land as Elyon's land. Elyon was just what we called it, nothing more. Flipping through its ragged pages was somehow comforting, and I began to think about having Grayson repair it so it would stop falling to pieces every time I picked it up. Lost in my thoughts, the clouds once again moved over the moon, and the blackness of the unlit night returned. Gusts of wind continued to blow; the first drops of rain pelted my hands on the sill, and I closed the book to protect it.

"Alexa!"

I jumped back from the window, lost my balance, and fell to the floor, all the while clutching the precious old book.

"Well, I guess that's one for me." It was Murphy climbing through the open window. His presence was a bad sign.

"Why are you here, Murphy? I need you to stay on the lookout," I said, getting back on my feet.

"That's just it, Alexa. I left an hour ago to check in with Yipes, and when I returned, it had been opened."

"Are you absolutely sure?" I asked. It appeared that my fears had come to pass.

"I'm positive. The chair was put back, but I marked the footings on the floor, and they no longer match up," said Murphy. He was staring at me wide eyed. "Either someone's got in through the secret door, or someone's got out. I can't be sure which."

A gust of wind slammed through the window and racked the shutters back and forth against the wall. Wind rushed into the room and blew Warvold's book clean out of my hand, bursting the spine loose anew and blowing pages all over the room.

"Oh no!" I cried. Some of the pages were sucked out the window as the wind changed directions, the rest were flying around the room in a blizzard of paper. I ran to the window and grabbed the shutters to close them. The rain was coming harder now and the handles on the shutters were slick. I saw pages from Warvolds book dancing on the wind outside. One was caught in the ivy clutches of the wall, another was stuck to the wet sill, and still another fluttered over the divide and out into the dark night beyond my site. I grabbed the page stuck to the sill and threw it behind me, then secured the shutters and turned to face the room.

It was worse than I thought possible. Pages were everywhere, and Murphy was dragging an empty spine across the floor by his teeth for my inspection. The book was forever destroyed.

"This is terrible, Murphy. We'll never get it back together, no matter how hard we try." He dropped the spine on my feet and looked up at me.

"I'm sorry."

I sat down with my back against the wall and Murphy hopped up on my lap. I picked up what was left of the book and opened it up. Not a single page remained. The spine was not only empty of pages, but torn at the stitching on the inside cover, revealing the inner board beneath the fabric. It had always been this way, at least ever since the book came into my possession. But with the pages gone the fault was more obvious and accessible. I ran my fingers along the edge absently, then, for no reason whatsoever, I tucked my finger under the fabric and felt along the board. It was a mindless gesture, and when I felt a ridge where one should not have been, I ignored it. Then I realized the ridge felt more like paper than board or fabric, and I looked closely at the broken cover. Something was inside. Something secret.

I looked at Murphy with astonishment, then I ripped the fabric off the cover and revealed a folded piece of paper. I set the mangled book aside and unfolded the treasure, my hands trembling with anticipation. It was one page, torn from Warvold's journal. The date and time of the entry indicated the night of his arrival in Bridewell for the summer meetings, probably between dinner and the stroll with me from which he never returned.

As the shutters buckled back and forth in opposition to the wind, I read the entry aloud to Murphy.

7/14 – 8pm
I have wondered ever since Renny was taken from me
if Sebastian is real. My arrival back in Bridewell makes

me wonder more than ever. Were Renny's suspicions imagined? 'He's not quite right' she would say upon our arrival. And who is this Sebastian anyway? Is he anything more than a mere legend heard in whispers? To tell the rest of them I must be utterly sure.

Grayson—I'm getting old and mischief follows me everywhere. If I am dead when you go to repair my favorite book (I know you won't be able to help yourself), you'll surely find this note. If events surrounding my death seem suspicious, read page 194. Otherwise, burn the book immediately and go about your day in peace.

W.

"Why did Grayson have to give me the book? For all we know page 194 is flying around outside somewhere!" I yelled. Murphy scrambled off my lap and began sifting through pages on the floor while I checked the one's that had landed on my bed. Five minutes into our search we were still looking, and all the pages in sight were piled in a heap in the corner of the room. It seemed likely that one of the pages outside, probably the one long gone over the wall, was the page we were looking for.

"Alexa!" came a muffled cry from under my bed, and a moment later Murphy came out, pushing page 194 along the floor with his nose, until I reached down and picked it up.

A moment later, with water pooling on my windowsill and dripping into the room, we huddled together in the corner near the pages we had piled up and I read page 194 aloud to Murphy.

We knew who Sebastian was, and Murphy said what we were both thinking.

"We have to catch him."

A Tight Spot

I unlocked my door and ran down the hall with Murphy close behind. When we arrived at the landing on the second floor, I stopped and gazed out the window toward the center of town where a shard of moonlight cut through the rain. The invasion had begun. As expected, the slaves had broken through a section of cobblestone in the main square, and they were boiling into Bridewell, one after another, lifting each other out of the hole. About thirty men were already inside the wall, crouching down, staying quiet and still until the rest of the men were inside. The rain began coming down in sheets, and the moon disappeared again behind ominous clouds, this time for the duration of the storm. I lost sight of the town square.

I would need a weapon, so I went to the kitchen and took the biggest knife I could find, and then I motioned Murphy in the direction of the library. On the way out of the kitchen I picked up a lamp from the table, lit it, and trimmed it so the flame was low.

As we crept down the dark hall, three explosions, one right after the other, erupted near the town square. The plan was fully engaged now, but it was impossible for me to know whether or not it was working.

We passed through the smoking room, went up the creaking steps, and stood at the landing in front of the library doors.

As I suspected, the doors had been locked from the inside, and the bookcase remained firmly backed against the wall in front of the cat door.

"I wonder if Sam and Pepper are still in there, watching for intruders," I said.

"If they are, then they're hiding." said Murphy. He hadn't seen them while he watched for activity in the library. We began to wonder if they might have jumped out the open window by the chair, but it was a long way down. Murphy could hold on and descend a twenty-foot wall, but the cats would have to freefall to the ground. No cat would willingly leap out a window that high.

The sound of thunderclaps and driving rain magnified the sinister darkness of Renny Lodge. I crouched down by the cat door and swung it toward me into the hall, inspecting the weight and size of the bookcase blocking the way. Already, there was almost enough room for Murphy to squeeze through, so I turned and put my foot through the small door against the bookcase. I pushed, just a little at first, then as hard as I could, but it would not budge. I held the door open with my hand, pulled my foot back, and waited for the next thunderclap. When it came, I thrust the flat of my heel into the bookcase. This produced a shooting pain up my leg, and the shelf remained in the exact same spot.

We sat motionless for a moment, and then without warning, Murphy moved quickly past my foot and sideways through the little door. He struggled mightily to squeeze into the small space as I spun around to where I could see.

He spoke in a muffled whisper I could hardly understand.

"Awfully tight in here. Can you push me through?"

I put my hand next to his furry side and started pushing. The wood against the back of the bookcase was slick, and his fur was soft, but the stone wall was rough. The coarseness of the wall combined with the slippery fur and wood made him twist as he went. I pushed, Murphy spun, alternately facing the stone wall, the exit, the bookcase, and me. It was hard not to laugh as I imagined his poor little face squashed against the wall, nose all flattened out, followed by a dazed look as he rotated free in my direction. I moved him as far as I could, but when my elbow reached the edge of the cat door, I could push no further, and Murphy was yet to reach the edge of the bookshelf.

He was stuck.

"Alexa?" he whispered.

"Yes?" I answered, the subtle beginnings of hysteria in my voice.

"Cat," he said.

And then I heard Sam's menacing laugh fill the library.

"How sad for you, Murphy—stuck in such an uncompromising position. And no one to save you," said Sam.

The time for quiet deliberation had passed, and I threw my full force into the library door over and over again trying to get in.

"It's no use, Alexa. He's finished, Bridewell is finished, and Sebastian has escaped undiscovered and unharmed. You have failed at every turn." This time it was Pepper, standing behind the door, taunting me.

I spun the knife in my hand and examined it, thinking of all that had gone wrong, and believing for a moment that I was defeated.

The cats were inspecting the bookcase, enjoying their little moment, continuing to taunt and jab as they decided who would rip into Murphy's flesh with a bare claw and yank him out.

"I think you should do the honors," joked Sam.

For no particular reason, I leaned against the library door, and continued examining the knife. It was a big knife with a solid wood handle and a wide blade.

"I almost wish I could let you in, Alexa. This is going to

be quite a sight to behold," said Pepper.

I quietly moved to the cat door and opened it.

"Enough of this. Get him out," said Sam.

I jammed the blade under the bookcase as hard as I could, and I lifted the handle up off the floor with all my strength. The bookcase tilted out slowly, then faster, then it was crashing into another shelf in front of it, spraying books everywhere. I could here shelves falling like dominoes out into the library, pounding the floor with books.

When all the shelves in the row had been toppled, I waited to hear the cats going after Murphy, but all I heard were random books slipping off of tipped shelves and popping on the floor like giant raindrops at the end of a storm.

Then I heard a magical sound. The lock on the library door creaked, and I watched as it slowly turned and snapped open. I carefully turned the handle and pushed the door open a few inches.

"Close call," said Murphy. He had already jumped down from the doorknob, and he was standing at my feet.

"Where are they?" I asked.

Murphy motioned me in and I followed him into the library. In the dim light it looked as though nine or ten shelves had tumbled over. Hanging out from under one of them were two lifeless cat tails.

"Oh my," I said. Murphy climbed over a bookshelf and started in the direction of the chair and the secret tunnel. I followed him into the dark recesses of the library.

SEBASTIAN

The shutters had not been closed and water was everywhere. Books, shelves, and the old chair—all were soaking wet. Rain continued to pour into the space as I pulled the chair back and revealed the secret entry. I removed the silver key from my pocket, unlocked the small door, and swung it open. A gust of wind blew it shut again with a bang and I worried over who might have heard from down below in the darkness.

I re-opened the door and held it tighter this time. The lamp that had hung on the ladder was gone, and I hung mine where it had been.

"Ready?" I asked Murphy. He nodded yes, and I picked him up and put him in my pack along with the knife. I descended the ladder as I had done before. When we arrived at the bottom, I released Murphy and set him on the dirt floor.

To my surprise, five of the boards that once lined the wall behind the ladder were strewn about the floor at my feet. Where the boards had been, the opening to an ominous dark corridor remained, staring at us like a giant black eye. I stepped through the opening and Murphy followed.

The brown walls reflected weak light from my lamp, and I had the creepy sense that Sebastian could jump out from a hiding spot at any moment and attack me. I turned the lamp down, just enough to see in front of me, and began running the length of the tunnel. After a while it turned and widened, and then I saw light flickering in the distance. I stopped and turned my lamp as low as I could and set it aside; then I sent Murphy ahead to scout the situation. He returned breathless and agitated. "We've reached the main tunnel. It shoots off in two directions, one back towards Bridewell by another route, and one out towards The Dark Hills. There's a torch lit at the corner. What do you want to do?"

Without answering I began running toward the flickering light as fast as I could. When I arrived at the torch I removed it from its holder and rammed it into the dirt floor until it was out. "What are you doing, Alexa?" yelled Murphy.

"Quiet down Murphy, you'll give us away," I whispered. I pulled a piece of paper from my sack, and held it down to the light. It was a crude copy of the map of the tunnels, something I thought I might find a use for after relinquishing the original.

"He would have tried to find his men, which means he would have taken this tunnel here," I pointed out a long, twisting black line that started from the hub we were standing at. "After that, he would intersect with this tunnel and drop down under Bridewell here," my finger followed along the map as I spoke. "If the explosives worked as they were meant to, then he would have encountered a dirt wall near the end, but that's a long way from here. To get all the way through the tunnels would have taken quite some time. And the only way back out is through the hub we're standing at." I paused a moment and looked at Murphy.

"He's separated from his men and looking for a way out. Either that, or he made it before the explosion," he concluded.

We sat motionless in the dark, the dim light from my lamp covered between my back and the wall of the cave. We waited quietly, which was difficult for Murphy. He kept flipping and flopping and then he started asking questions.

"If the explosions closed off the tunnels, then the slaves are trapped in Bridewell. I'm not sure that's a good plan with so many slaves to deal with," he whispered.

Before I could respond, we both saw a flicker of light coming from out of the darkness. It was moving fast. I hunkered down at the edge of the adjoining tunnel and pulled the knife from my pack. The light bounced brighter and brighter off the walls, and then the shadow of a man came into view. I could hear his labored breathing and his steps as he moved across the dirt floor. Thunder clapped from outside in a muffled tone, and I peeked around the corner to see how close he was. Only about ten yards off, Sebastian had slowed to a brisk walk. I slipped back into the darkness, and as he passed in front of me I thrust as hard as I could and drove the knife into the fleshy part of his calf. He screamed in pain and threw his lamp to the ground, hopping on one leg over to the side of the tunnel with his back to me, holding himself up with one hand. Blood was streaming down his leg in a sheet of red.

I picked up my lamp and turned it up, holding the knife in one hand. Sebastian, still turned away from me, winced in pain, his hand over the wound trying to stop the flow of blood.

"You stupid girl!" He shouted, throwing a handful of loose dirt into my face. I was blinded but kept a firm grip on the knife as I went down and tried to rub the dust out of my eyes. I felt a forceful blow to my ribs and the wind was knocked out of me. Then I was thrown over on my back and the knife was wrenched out of my hands. I waited for the impact of the blade against my skin. Instead I heard a voice.

"If you follow me one step further, I'll drive this knife into your heart," he whispered, grotesquely close to my ear, dripping sweat in my hair. Then he moved away from me and I heard the sound of smashing glass as he destroyed my lamp.

"He's got the light and the knife and he's heading for The

Dark Hills," yelled Murphy. I could hear Sebastian dragging his bad leg as he went. I sat up and tried desperately to clean the dirt out of my eyes. They stung badly, and I could only see a blurry view of the light dancing off into the distance.

"I have no weapon and no light, and I can hardly see. This is going well wouldn't you say?"

"We can catch him if we hurry," countered Murphy. He raced down the tunnel before I could stop him, so I followed as fast as I could. My ribs were on fire where Sebastian had kicked me, and I was having trouble catching my breath. Another fifty yards and I'd be finished. The light was getting closer again as I rounded a corner and slowed down. I crept a little farther, and saw that Sebastian was in a familiar underground room. The map of the tunnels hung on the wall and he was studying it, looking for the way out.

I knew this room.

I crept in behind him against the wall and looked all around for some sort of weapon I could use. A lighted torch was all I could find, and I quietly moved towards it. Murphy hid in the shadows and waited.

"I told you not to follow me," said Sebastian. His voice shocked me, and I stumbled over my feet, landing beneath the torch. He remained with his back to me, unmoving.

"I wouldn't have believed it was you if not for the clues that were left behind," I said, my voice shaking with fear. "Renny had you figured out first, but Warvold had to be convinced. The clues he left me led to a page in his favorite book describing a mythical elephant god from a fanciful story set on the other side of Mount Laythen at the edge of the sea." I stood up and groped along the wall for the torch.

"An imaginary god called Ganesh."

There was a long moment of silence in the room. I pulled my hand away from the torch and waited, not sure what he would do. He remained facing away from me, and began to speak in a tired old voice.

"I was lazy, brash, and I didn't want to work. In Ainsworth a young man with those characteristics had better either shape up or leave town," he said. Then he turned and looked at me for the first time with his hollow eyes, old before their time. "I did neither, and by the time I was nineteen, I had this." He pulled his shirt aside and revealed a 'V' branded to his chest. *'V' is for Vagabond* the thought kept racing through my head.

"On the inside, we joked that the 'V' was for Victory, but the guards in Ainsworth were ruthless. A few vagabonds were killed; many others were beaten within an inch of their lives. If Warvold had not come along, I am quite sure we would all be long since dead." He shuffled closer with his injured leg and stood before me.

"But he did emerge, and the officials in Ainsworth were thrilled to rid themselves of us. Warvold was no softy, but as long as we worked hard and obeyed, he took care of us. We ate well, worked hard, and enjoyed a bed to sleep in at night. For many of us, this was as good a life as we'd ever known." Ganesh turned my knife in his hand and examined it absently. There was a strange, leisurely madness about him.

"When the wall was finished, Warvold and his guards escorted us back to Ainsworth as promised. We were all thirty or thirty-five years old by then, beaten down from years of hard labor. We were no longer strong-willed, able young men, and this terrified us.

"Ainsworth never expected Warvold to return us, and they surely didn't plan for it. After a week of life back in the prison I thought I might go insane. The place was full when we got there, and we nearly doubled the number overnight.

"I talked with one of the guards, and I told him if they released all of the slaves that had worked in Bridewell into the wilderness, I could guarantee that no one would ever see or hear from us again. We would remain in the wild where no one would find us, and if any of us were found, we would expect nothing short of death. Seeing this as a way to rid themselves of us once and for all without having to kill us, the officials agreed to the plan, and shortly after that, under cover of night, they released us into The Dark Hills." He was growing weary from blood loss, rocking back and forth and catching himself like a drunk, but he was determined to finish the story.

"Once released, we began planning a takeover of the walled city. Bridewell is a marvelous fortress, and with it under our control, we could bargain with Ainsworth as equals, and turn Bridewell into a trade route between Ainsworth and the sea towns of Turlock and Lathbury.

"Warvold never allowed beards for obvious reasons, but it wasn't long before we all had them. Those of us with brands on our cheeks hoped to cover them up. Mine was conveniently low, and my beard grew very thick, so I was an obvious choice to send out.

"Shortly after our arrival in The Dark Hills, I moved to Turlock. It had just been settled, and only a few hundred people lived there. I immediately went to work on houses and other buildings, and I involved myself in all forms of planning for the town. Within a year, it grew to several thousand people, and I was elected Mayor. With no family to speak of, working sometimes twenty hours a day to build the community, I was a natural selection.

"The rest is fairly obvious. You know all about talking to animals, so there's no sense my hiding it now. Some of our slaves discovered the pool and its strange powers. They befriended the hawk, and the hawk befriended the cats.

"I began making trips to Bridewell and started planning the invasion. We needed information that would take time to attain, and there was a lot of work to expand the already extensive tunnel system. But here we are, seven years later, and the invasion is upon us."

"What will you do now?" I questioned, trying to keep him talking. "You're cut off from your men, wounded, and found out."

Ganesh looked at me with a cold stare, the knife glistening in his hand, blood oozing down his damaged leg. "It's refreshing to cleanse the soul in telling my story, but the situation remains obvious: nobody else knows I'm down here, and there are a lot of ways out. I'll have to kill you, just like I killed Warvold. With him it was poison, not too messy. With you I'm afraid I'll have to draw some blood." I leapt for the torch and grabbed a hold with both hands, waving it in front of me.

"You really think that dried out piece of wood is going to save you? I think not." His mood had turned dark and threatening. This was not Ganesh; this was Sebastian. He advanced on me and I began to move around the room to one side, swishing the flame back and forth between us as I went.

He was just close enough to bat the torch out of my hands and drive the knife into me when Murphy darted out of the shadows, jumped onto Sebastian's leg, and chomped down with all his force, driving his teeth deep into flesh. Sebastian screamed fiercely, looked down, and with one brute swing batted Murphy across the room. I was up against the wall opposite the map, nowhere to hide, and Sebastian, fuming with rage, focused all of his years of anger squarely on me. He advanced quickly, ripped the flaming torch from my hands, and pinned me to the wall with his forearm.

"Aaaaarrrrgggggh!" He screamed and pulled back to drive the knife into me. I closed my eyes and waited for the impact.

But the impact never came. I heard the sound of wood splintering and I was thrown to the ground. Dirt flew everywhere and I lost sight of Sebastian altogether.

"Murphy, what have you done?" I slid down against the wall and held my knees to my chest.

As the dust settled to the ground I saw Sebastian, a huge knife sticking out of his chest, laying flat on the ground. Standing over him, covered in dirt from top to bottom, was a little man. Next to him was Darius, dripping saliva, his massive gaping mouth hovering ominously over Sebastian's neck, ready to drive razor sharp teeth into flesh upon the slightest movement from Sebastian's body.

"Yipes!" I screamed. I jumped up and grabbed him around the waist, hugging him mercilessly. Then I turned to Darius, touched his ominous head, and pulled him close.

"It's all right now. It's all right," said Yipes. I looked back over my head and saw that Yipes and Darius had crashed though the hiding spot, a big gaping hole where once there was dirt wall. Splintered boards dangled aimlessly into the air of the chamber.

"How did you know?" I said.

"Just a hunch, a hunch is all," he said. "But Darius is the real hero. He overcame unthinkable fear to crawl down the tunnel and make sure you were safe. The big brute barely fit. Without him I could not have broken through the wall. He's as strong as an ox."

Murphy came hobbling up beside us. He seemed dazed but unharmed.

"Good to see you all back together again," he said. And then, in a comic whisper to Yipes, "Keep an eye on her old boy, she's got a reputation for throwing us small ones around."

Yipes reached into his vest pocket and pulled out a small, sharp looking knife. He approached Sebastian with caution, turned his lifeless head to the side, and placed the edge of the knife against his face. He looked back at me and motioned me closer, then he pulled down on the knife and revealed the dark crest of the letter 'S' beneath Sebastian's thick beard.

"I guess that settles it for good."

I could hardly hear him say it, and then I was adrift somewhere far away where no one could find me, deeper into the tunnels, all the way out under The Dark Hills and into darker tunnels still, until I was so far and deep I could never be found again. And it was very dark indeed.

"Wake up, Alexa. Wake up."

I felt as though pulled by a cord out into the light, and I awoke to see my father's familiar, comforting eyes staring down at me. I reached up and grabbed him around the neck. Even with the pain in my side, I held him longer and tighter than I ever had before.

"You passed out," he said. "Yipes tried to revive you, but couldn't. He came looking for help in Bridewell."

I looked over and saw that Pervis was inspecting Sebastian's dead body, and then it occurred to me for the first time what had happened. Yipes had been in Bridewell, with people—civilized people—which meant it was only a matter of time before he would lose his gift to speak with animals.

"It can't be," I said. "Please say you didn't do it." I reached for his hand and he took mine, but he wouldn't look at me.

"It's been worth it, Alexa, really it has," he said. "It's all been worth it. Besides, I have a good feeling things were about to change out there anyway. This just speeds things up a bit."

I held onto his tiny hand a long time, my eyes filling with tears, and I whispered quietly: "Thank you."

Murphy came over and jumped up into the new opening that led out into the wild, and he balanced on one of the boards that had been broken free. Darius was nowhere to be seen. His fear of tunnels overcome, I could only assume that he had rushed home to reunite with his family.

"Come on Yipes, it's time for us to go," said Murphy.

I nodded my approval and let go of Yipes' hand.

"We'll see each other again," he said, and then he hopped up into the hole and I watched him vanish into the darkness. Murphy re-appeared, leapt from the edge of the hole, and landed confidently in my outstretched arms.

"You're a hero," he said. "Not quite the hero I am, but a hero nonetheless." I held him close, rose to my feet and set him in the hole, and then he too was gone.

"We've got to get above ground, Alexa. I think you'll be surprised by what you see," said Pervis.

We left the small, dingy room with its gaping wound, my father on one side and Pervis on the other. It was comforting to have them with me.

"Who's the rodent?" said Pervis, putting his arm around my shoulder.

"He's a squirrel actually, a good one. Talks a little too much, but a nice fellow."

Pervis laughed heartily and I managed a smile. He had no idea that I was being perfectly truthful.

BEYOND BRIDEWELL

T hings had progressed dramatically in the town square while I was busy chasing Sebastian through the underground tunnels, and it looked as though our plan had worked. The town square was a sight to behold.

For the previous two days, every able-bodied man in Bridewell had worked tirelessly to build a wall within a wall. We knew the slaves would come from The Dark Hills side, and so, stone by stone, the top half of the wall separating Bridewell from the forest was taken down and put back together again twenty feet high, all the way around the town square.

As soon as all the slaves were inside, ready to pounce on Bridewell in the stormy black night, the explosions were set off at locations coinciding with the map. Three detonations were used to be sure the tunnel would cave in and trap the slaves, a few below ground, but most already out of the tunnel, completely unaware of the trick that had been played on them.

"The darkness and the storm helped us even more," said Pervis as we approached the wall and the muted sound of men inside, trapped like mice in a cage. "Some of the slaves ran smack into the wall before they ever saw it around them. At first, they acted confused and huddled together near the center. That's when we figured they were all out of the tunnel, and we set off the explosions and turned on the lamps." Pervis walked me over to one of the rain soaked ladders and pointed up. "I think you should go and take a look," he said.

It was a victorious moment, and even with the pain shooting through my side, I was on the ladder climbing without hesitation. It was twenty rungs up, and as I took one painful stride after another, rain pelting my face, I was reminded of climbing the ladder out of the library tunnel, the big wooden door blowing open over my head, the excitement I had felt.

When I reached the top and looked out over the edge inside the stone prison we'd built, I cleared my eyes of rain again and again, sure that what I was seeing had to be wrong.

I looked down to Pervis and yelled through the rain: "What's going on Pervis? Have they retreated into the tunnel?"

Pervis looked up at me for a long, silent moment, then yelled back: "We've sent men in to check, Alexa, and that's all there is. Nicholas is with one of them now in the smoking room, gathering more information."

It just wasn't possible. Huddled in the pouring rain like shimmering black boulders, were about fifty pitiful looking men. Guards on all sides pinned them down, and the hole from where they had emerged was being filled in with mud and rocks by another group of Bridewell men.

I looked back down at Pervis in the driving rain and yelled: "Where did they all go?"

Pervis looked up at me, blocking the rain from his eyes with one hand. "They're all dead, Alexa. Most have been dead a long time. The ones in there are all that remain, and most of them are so weak they can barely hold a weapon. Come on down from there, I can hardly see you through this rain." He began waving me down from the ladder.

I took a long last look, and some of them looked back at me. One waved and produced a sickly smile, raising his eyebrows as if to say 'I'm nice, really I am. Can we be friends?'

I descended the ladder with mud-covered shoes, soaking wet and tired, and stood before Pervis.

"Why the gash on your forehead? Don't tell me one of them actually took a swipe at you," I said. He touched his temple with his hand and wiped away some of the watery blood, grimacing as he did so.

"Slipped on a rung and bashed my head against the wall coming down." He placed his hand against one of the massive stones in the structure we'd just spend two days building. "It seems as though the only things causing pain around here are these ridiculous walls we keep building."

As it turned out, there were fifty-seven slaves who tried to invade Bridewell that night. Men who had never known a good home, never understood who to trust or how to overcome adversity. All the rest had died waiting for Sebastian or Ganesh or whomever he was to give them orders to attack. He had taken terrible advantage of their willingness to follow blindly if someone, anyone, would just lead them. While he lived a life of royalty for seven long years, they hid in tunnels; scrounged for food, missed the chance to have families of their own, and watched their friends die of disease. Most of them were barely adults when they entered the prison at Ainsworth, and cowering there in the town square that night, I got the feeling they only wanted a place they could call home. I was scared to death of what was to become of them. But I needn't have worried.

A few days later, after things calmed down, my father and Nicholas decided to send twenty of the remaining slaves to Lunenburg, twenty to Turlock, and seventeen to Lathbury. They were assimilated into our society not as slaves or savages, but as servants, living with families and given a chance for a fresh start. None have ever returned to a life of crime, and many have families of their own now.

A few days after the servants were released, my father and I took a group of men to the midway point on the road from Bridewell to Lathbury, and we smashed six-foot holes in the walls on both sides of the road. Before we left, I walked out into the forest with my father and watched as Darius came into view, peeking out from behind a tree. Then two more wolves crept out behind him, Odessa and Sherwin. I waved and the three of them howled: thank you. That was the last thing I ever understood an animal say.

A year after the so-called invasion, the people of Bridewell voted to tear down the walls. Two years after that, the giant blocks that once formed the massive walls were strewn across the valley floor in thousands of pieces, weeds and flowers alike growing between the shattered stones, like an endless broken tombstone.

Now, when I make the trip from Lathbury to Bridewell, I see animals all along the way. I no longer understand what they say, and it makes me feel old, like all the child has gone out of me. But I still get a funny look now and then from a squirrel or a wolf or a fox, and I remember the thrill of those days and all that was at stake, so much that nobody will ever know or understand, and for a passing moment I feel like I'm twelve again, the magic filling the forest, and I can almost hear them talking.

Pervis and Grayson remain residents of Bridewell. I visit them every summer, as I always have, and I bring strawberries. Pervis is still the head guard, and with the walls down, he seems a tad more jumpy, forever casting a wary eye toward Ainsworth. But he has also mellowed, and when I visit we stroll the nights away and talk about that one amazing summer. Every visit I spend hours and hours in the library, walking the aisles of books, looking for the volume I've missed that would make for the perfect summer companion. Grayson and I sit quietly reading all day, sometimes nodding off to sleep, other times sharing a favorite passage, like only old friends can.

Yipes moved to Lathbury for almost a year, but he missed the wild of the mountains so much he returned to his house on the river. I bring him buckets of tomatoes from my mother's garden in the summer, and blankets from the country store in the winter. He seems content to live out his days mostly alone, and he goes back to the pool and looks for stones once every year. I know, because I go with him and I look too, but we never find any. The ones we find are as dull and lifeless as the one I carry in a leather pouch around my neck.

In fact, as far as I can tell, all of Elyon's magic has drained out of the valley, leaving a dry and barren void even when the rainy season is upon us. I suppose the wall had its own way of holding the enchanting beauty of the wild away from us for a time, but eventually we found a way to snuff out what little magic remained. Maybe that's just what people do, or maybe Elyon, if he's real at all, is getting further away from us as Ander had suggested in the forest. How I wished I had pushed Ander for more answers when I had had the chance. I feared the great silence between us would forever make Elyon a mystery to me.

Lately I've been wondering whether or not I could go off searching for a place where you could stand in a pool of icy water and come out talking to animals. A place where secret messages could be found, and squirrels are full of comic bravery. Sometimes I think I could ask Yipes and he would go with me, and we could travel the world just like Warvold did, looking for pockets of magic where Elyon's presence still remained. But then I'm not twelve anymore, and sometimes I'm almost sure adventures like that only happen when you're a child.

I see servants wherever I go, and I hope they won't see me. But they always do, and they talk with me about that summer, about a lot of other things. I always experience the same anxious feeling whenever they approach, a mix of excitement and dread at reliving their painful past, and a heaving weight on my chest. Memories fade, but a mark from a hot iron remains, and so I talk with them for as long as they want, listening to their stories. After a while, the passing of time will wash the brands away, the generations scrubbing our collective memories as the last of them die off.

But today is a good day. I'm on my way to the Bridewell library to deliver this story, a story that took me three years to finish. Maybe a child will wander into the library a hundred years from now, read my story, and it will be a little harder for everyone to forget the past.

I wonder what would happen if I drove my cart through Bridewell, onto Ainsworth, and beyond—a girl of fifteen and not a wall in sight to hold me back. Was that a rabbit that just winked at me? I think I just saw Ander in the mist, and I hear Darius howling through the wind swept trees. Could it be that Elyon is in the shadows, waiting for us, longing to be with us once again? Maybe an unscheduled visit to see Yipes with a big bag of tomatoes would be a good idea after all.

Author's Notes

The Dark Hills Divide was originally constructed as a weekly serial for the author's two daughters. If you should run across them in your travels, cover your ears and run the other way. They are talkative little darlings and we are always somewhere beyond the reader in Alexa's adventures.

Bridewell was a real place; a prison in England, where they really did brand 'V's on vagabonds.

Renny Lodge was the name of one of the buildings at the historic Bridewell prison.

Lathbury (the first town Warvold settled) is a town from the Robert Frost poem "The Mountain."

The Grob is a genuine chess strategy used for precisely the reasons outlined in this story.

Cabeza de Vaca (old cow head) was a real person, a Spanish explorer from the fifteenth century.

Coming Soon

THE LAND OF ELYON BOOK 2

BEYOND THE VALLEY OF THORNS

Alexa Daley has been keeping quiet, living out what remains of her life in the city of Lathbury, mending books and daydreaming about far away places. But all that changes when a mysterious letter arrives from an old friend beckoning her to the slave caves, a dark and ominous place, the one place she doesn't want to go.

Thus begins the second installment in The Land of Elyon series, in which Alexa leaves the safe confines of Bridewell Common and travels into The Dark Hills and beyond. She discovers stunning new lands, finds extraordinary new friends, and encounters a strange new evil with the power to destroy The Land of Elyon.

Full of excitement and peril, Beyond the Valley of Thorns will redefine everything Alexa believes about the world she inhabits. She will discover the dark, unseen forces at work all around her, and she will carry a burden she alone was meant for, a burden that will determine the fate of The Land of Elyon and all who reside there.